PRAISE FOR INÊS PEDROSA

Praise for *Still I Miss You*

"*Still I Miss You* is a marvelous novel, a ballad of disenchantment."

—*Diário de Notícias* (Portugal)

"Amidst the triumph of the commonplace, this novel by Inês Pedrosa is a mad torrent, a thread of light, a storm to which no one could remain immune or indifferent."

—*Grande Reportagem* (Portugal)

"This book is all about a mystery made sublime by the author's writing, in a meticulously crafted and virtually mirrored web of intrigue . . . A beautiful novel, with a desire to change the world, and which, besides everything else, one reads effortlessly, unable to stop."

—*Expresso* (Portugal)

"Inês Pedrosa has enjoyed such tremendous success with her novels because her themes—brimming with powerful emotions, human frailties, and the misunderstandings of existence—grab hold of readers page by page, allowing them to lose themselves completely."

—*Oggi* (Italy)

"*Still I Miss You* demonstrates all the literary gifts of this author who, born in 1962, embodies the new post-Saramago and post–Lobo Antunes literature of Portugal. The novel is a heartbreaking tale of love, abruptly ended, but recovered in the voice of the woman who has suddenly died, a literary conceit demanding total mastery."

—*Bravo!* (Brazil)

Praise for *In Your Hands*

"This novel by a prizewinning Portuguese journalist intertwines the political and the personal through its incantatory prose . . . Absorbing in its history, as well as in its family dynamics."

—*New York Times Book Review*

"This passionate, resonant novel is now in English for the first time."

—*Philadelphia Inquirer*

"*In Your Hands* is another work in the fine tradition of European literature. Told from a definite feminist perspective, it focuses on the inner feelings of its principal characters, each a finely drawn and vital woman, as they navigate the turbulent times of twentieth-century Portugal."

—*Writers & Readers Magazine*

"Pedrosa's extraordinary prose is colorful, thought-provoking, and emotionally rich. This is a novel that rewards the reader on every page with the thrill of great storytelling and the satisfaction of deeply etched characters whose lives are indelibly marked by the legacy of a forsaken love."

—*Words Without Borders*

"Portugal through a woman's voice is Amália Rodrigues with her divinely nostalgic fados; and now it's likewise Inês Pedrosa in this, her powerfully evocative, but no less heartrending novel *In Your Hands*."

—Laura Restrepo, author of *Delirium* and *Hot Sur*

"This beautiful, philosophical novel—lyrical, passionate, alert to the ways in which history shapes us—is also a profound meditation on love. Pedrosa writes about the romance between an unconventional woman and her wayward husband, about two men who loved each other at a time when such love was taboo, and about the love that connects three generations of Portuguese women who manage to flourish as human beings despite the horrors of dictatorship and Portugal's colonial legacy. Inês Pedrosa is a great novelist in the tradition of the Brontës, Virginia Woolf, Simone de Beauvoir, and another singular writer who also writes in Portuguese—Clarice Lispector. *In Your Hands* is filled with wisdom and beauty like few novels I know."

—Jaime Manrique, author of *Latin Moon in Manhattan* and *Cervantes Street*

"A wonderfully poetic novel, in which you can immerse yourself with pleasure."

—*Brigitte* (Germany)

"The author succeeds in conjuring up powerful emotions for a wide audience while at the same time pursuing her aesthetic and political objectives."

—*Die Zeit* (Germany)

"Inês Pedrosa's writing leaves us completely in her hands."

—*Em Frente Oeste* (Portugal)

"[Pedrosa] has focused on the inner feelings and emotions [of her characters], illuminating them with her prose, exploring their tensions and conflicts."

—*El País* (Spain)

Still I Miss You

ALSO BY INÊS PEDROSA

In Your Hands

Still I Miss You

Inês Pedrosa

Translated by ANDREA ROSENBERG

amazoncrossing

Previously published as *Fazes me falta* by Dom Quixote in Portugal in 2006. Translated from Portuguese by Andrea Rosenberg. First published in English by AmazonCrossing in 2019.

Quote from Luís Filipe Castro Mendes's "A Ilha dos Mortos" reprinted by permission of the author.

Two short quotations from Graham Greene's *The End of the Affair*: New York: The Viking Press, 1951, by permission of Penguin Random House, New York. Copyright © Graham Greene, 1951; Copyright renewed Graham Greene, 1979.

Published by AmazonCrossing, Seattle

www.apub.com

Amazon, the Amazon logo, and AmazonCrossing are trademarks of Amazon.com, Inc., or its affiliates.

ISBN-13: 9781542093330 (hardcover)
ISBN-10: 1542093333 (hardcover)
ISBN-13: 9781542044417 (paperback)
ISBN-10: 1542044413 (paperback)

Cover design by Philip Pascuzzo

Printed in the United States of America

First edition

In memory of my father, Ricardo Pedrosa.
For Nelson de Matos and José Francisco Feiçao,
my companions in undying nostalgia.

Happy for having everything I am.
Happy for losing all I've ever known.

Only I can't give you what I will no longer be.
No, my death, I cannot give it to you.

Pedro Tamen

1

Dying isn't enough to get you a glimpse of God's smile—even if, like me, you've spent your entire life basking in it. When the worst happened, that smile descended into my darkness with a swing's sobbing lament, a swaying of hinges pulled from the chains of childhood. I sat on it and rose, swinging, toward the light. I was lucky: the worst happened to me early. God embraces first those who suffer before having any concrete knowledge of pain, maybe because everybody else knows too much to be able to be saved.

You used to say it was just the opposite: that God is born of the ignorance that characterizes premature suffering. But you, my favorite student, were quickly inhabited by an excess of knowledge. God didn't know anything about the universe when he created it. I imagine he must have been lonely. I imagine that, at a certain point, that loneliness must have become larger than God himself, bursting into an enormous bloom of light. And I imagine him, afterward, trying to make sense of each petal of that scattered light. Now that I've left the body that used to be me—now become pollen, dust in your eyes, pure imagination—I can imagine it even better, drunk on light, lucid, dazzled by a hidden Lucifer, a creative Lucifer embedded in his own being, in a state of passion, with all of history unleashed by his omnipotent solitude. And I soar within his smile once more, for good this time, since my body is lying supine down there, in a coffin, being contemplated and remembered and mourned for the last time.

I won't be getting out of bed tomorrow after asking in a muffled voice for him to give the swing a bigger push, to push hard till my feet fly beyond the grounded warmth of the bedsheets. Nobody else will be waiting for me; I won't have to wrap myself in apologies; I'll never deceive or disillusion anybody again. I won't be going back to die in the body of the only man who ever opened the secret passageway to death inside me. I won't be returning to the disappointment of rebirth. Most of all, I will never disappoint you again—you, unbeliever who taught me to believe better, my ancient, pocket-size god, my friend.

Stripped of my body, I more easily transform into the swing, into the dancing light it's made of. In a whisper of wind, I implore him not to push me so swiftly toward that illuminated place that is His Flesh; I implore him to let me take one last breath here, linger a little longer in the world I left so suddenly. A little longer near you. Or take your last breath, the way children do, so I can start over with another story in the everyday oscillation of your smile.

Only your laughter remains. I showed you the sea.

I showed it to you before and after your death.

Luís Filipe Castro Mendes

1

I'm alone. Alone with my heart shattered into pieces by visions of you. I can no longer offer you my heart on a silver platter. Did I ever want it? Did you? What I need now is some sort of god to act as my messenger boy. A god who would stroke your hair and remind me how soft it was. A god who'd free me from this persistent image of your body in a box. Remember how you always used to laugh at what you called my "compulsive boxification"? "One of these days, I'm going to come in and find you in the middle of a rising tide of papers, totally exhausted, about to drop dead. But there's no way I'm boxing you up—dead bodies freak me out."

I always told you fear attracts misfortune—go ahead and laugh. Laugh all you want now; nobody can hear you. Go on—if your God exists, let out a big belly laugh and prove it to me. Actually, no, don't: a posthumous chortle would spoil my beautiful archive of your laughter. It would screw up the aesthetics, you know? And aesthetics, frankly, were never your strong suit. You couldn't stand fakery. You hated the knee-jerk rejection of life's paradoxes. Your death is a perfect example—couldn't you have died of something less bizarre? Held out for the dignity of your first wrinkles? What a penchant for kitsch you had, my dear—but God always manifests himself in kitsch, doesn't he?

Rest in peace. You made a pretty corpse—prettier and more serene than you ever were in life, kid. They touched up your image. Public figures live—and die—by their image. Image über alles. Maybe it would have been better if I hadn't seen you, hadn't kissed your forehead. I clung to that last trace of your warmth. You left me with the lingering scent of incense and dead flowers. The fragrance of the forbidden love we left scattered across the landscape of our prehistoric past. I call it love for simplicity's sake. Some words are like that; we use them as a way of calming ourselves. Rattle them off to keep ourselves from thinking. What used to exist, what still exists between us is a science of disappearance. I started to disappear the day my eyes dove into yours. Now that your eyes are closed for good, I know you'll never give mine back.

In that story that no longer includes me, the story I rode like a carousel, the story that is always only a temporary dwelling place, people have questions. What sense does it make for a thirty-seven-year-old woman to die, damn it, destroyed by her own posterity? You'd quit smoking so you wouldn't die of cancer. It wasn't death itself you were worried about, you said, but the meandering of it, the torment of illness. The story. I don't think I ever saw you sick—except with love. You nurtured the vice of passion with methodical implacability. You always ran counterclockwise. You sought the motionlessness of a stone-carved time that was already yours. Or ours—but how could we ever say that, when we had to keep on living? During those brief periods when you weren't in a relationship, you became unbearable. You weren't excited about anything. Later, when you started a career in the halls of power, you lost that tendency toward romantic ecstasy. You shifted into storytelling, the soothing burble of gossip. Even your wardrobe changed—the last few times I saw you, you were wearing these horrible power suits, clumsily cut and sewn Armani knockoffs, in garish grays. "Wow, check out the business-lady get-up!" I said, and you explained it was just for work. On the weekends, you said, you went back to your usual style. But style is a way of being, not a weekend outfit. Politics robbed you of your style and stole you from me. Politicians don't need friends, they need a retinue—it's textbook. You went to your life and I to mine. As you know, I live my life in flashes of lightning; the thunder you and I shared rumbled on a little longer than usual—that's all. Anyway, death hovers over the joys of that chronology we seized on in an effort to escape the bounds of time. What are we beyond what we're actually being? You were my beyond—the magnet of my intimate, impersonal temporality. Redemption from the evils that amputated me. You. Now pure vapor of the universe. You're like God for me now—who could have imagined it? I turn to you for what I do not know how to be, and that's the truth. I look out at the sea at Guincho Beach, at those cold, fierce waves you relished diving into, and I, too, feel like I'm half dead, half cold. Happy to be by your side again. Beside the woman who was already dead a good couple of years before you died. I miss you. But life, ultimately, is just all those absences that drive us. Your death has allayed my fear of dying. With you out of the game, I'm less interested in the whole ordeal. And since you've died, I, too, will be capable of dying, without disturbing the waves or the sky or the silence. Falling into you, further and further from the pathetic fiction of me.

2

God pushes slower, allowing me to revisit the city I loved so much with you. Little things: in the yard beside your house, a boy is spreading his wings in the middle of a flock of gray pigeons, which stir and leave him behind down there, still flapping. There's a young woman pacing back and forth, watching the boy and talking on her cell phone: "You're a dick. I don't give a crap, you're a fucking dick. Your son's going to figure out what a dick of a father he's got."

When I was dying, I didn't see green valleys or my life in slow motion, didn't hear celestial music. Maybe it's possible to die like that, the way I've heard it described so often. Maybe it's even possible that, in the final moment, the lightning bolt of genius might place a few redemptive words in one's mouth. I always doubted it, but all our doubts are possible, I think, now that I no longer have the supreme pleasure of doubting. Death is a secret text, the only one whose copyright the author has not relinquished. I can tell you about my death, here in this space without space, because God knows you're no longer able to hear me. But I know you're imagining it in countless different ways and that, because of those imaginings, all those deaths of mine exist in this intimate space of nonexistence.

I died in an echo, reduplicated. I died when a drifter got lost on the way to my uterus; I died because my body decided to produce a new life and screwed it up. I saw death open the floodgates of my blood, but it was only at the end of that red river that I saw I'd been carrying an impossible child. The first sensation I experienced, after passing out from the pain, was the intense smell of infant, the hot, sour scent of vomited milk. The swing of God's smile suddenly caught me in a gash of light, and resting on my thighs was a sort of tiny baby, practically just a baby's smile that seemed to have emerged straight from my belly onto my lap. A seed, a stone, a warm thing emanating happiness, stripping away my pain. And then undone in a blue light, with a sigh of relief. Then the swing became weightless and started spinning for what seemed like an eternity inside a rose of white light. The waves of light of that spiraling rose explained everything I didn't know about my death, and much of what I'd forgotten about my life. Simple things, like that child I'd been producing in an unviable part of my body, in the blind wisdom of unawareness. And things even simpler than that, ineffable things, like the snags in the fabric of my friendship with you. Irremediable, tranquil things. My God, let me perfect in them the first concert of my eternity. He softened the heat of his smile, the solar petals of the rose I was climbing retreated, and I, now only a breath of wind, slowly descended over our city.

My perspective wasn't that vantage of intelligent disdain learned in airplane windows, no. I already suspected that the rectangular glance we cast over the frenzied movements of human ants bears no resemblance to the compassionate tilt of God's gaze. In this first pleat of transcendence, in this nolus in the gap between your time and my eternity, my orbitless gaze fixes on maximal enlargements of minimal details. From the child trying to be a pigeon to the closed windows of your house, which lies empty because you've gone to sit with my body. You've left the bathroom light on, the wardrobe doors flung open, and a pair of dark-red briefs balled up on the floor beside the bed. How unlike you.

2

Did you think about me as you were dying? I'd pay a lot of money to know the answer to that—as long as it was true. Because the truth does exist—everything's not all relative like you insisted. There is a truth, and that's what united us—that there was truth, a steadfast ship. Some people agreed with us, but at a distance. The distance of conviviality and cocktails that became a new intimacy. For you, the truth was never out of reach—were you already with me on that childhood morning when I tried to swim out to the ship of the horizon? They fished me out before I got there, with a rowboat and a couple of sharp slaps—are you nuts, kid?

A person lives better, or so I'm told, when he invents the truth every day. Pretend you haven't died. Just pretend. The two of us tried to invent everything but the truth. Even when the truth was our enemy. Especially when it was our enemy. We wanted to kill bad truth and spread good truth—are we nuts, kid?

How can I kill your death? In dreams, you come looking for me, take me with you down a long, dark corridor. Why are there so many corridors in our dreams, and all of them so dark? But in the end you look at me, and it's no longer you. A skull with scraps of flesh in its eye sockets laughs at me and goes neener-neener-neener the way kids do—ha ha, fooled you. When I wake up, I have a hard time separating you from the skull. I see your bones, nerves, and decaying skin in pictures of you, a caustic smile floating in the silence of the room. And everything reeks of old age, the instant putrefaction you became. You didn't want me to see you dead—is that why you're punishing me?

Seeking the truth turns us into punishers. I tripped over your little lies so often. They stung me deeply. I'd lie right back, a little more vehemently, so you'd notice. Lies. You took a witticism that had been mine and made it yours, and that anecdote found its way back to me, expanded, made meaner by bits of humor you'd added at my expense. You weren't like that when we met. You used to quote me. With quotation marks and everything. Your charm lay in the way— the exceedingly rare way—that quote marks shone around your statements. "So-and-so told me," you'd say. "What's-his-head said." You highlighted the insight and beauty of other people's words. Once you went into politics, you shed that precision like an uncomfortable skin. The names were eclipsed, swept beneath the solemn rug of "reliable sources." Later, as you gained confidence, you eventually did away entirely with citing sources. So many sentences that left my lips for your ears, crafted for the purpose of making you laugh, made their way back to me in the newspapers, as "quotes of the week" that had issued from your noble brain.

That's not to say I question the brilliance and vastness of your intelligence. You were an existential doctoral dissertation in motion. Did I ever tell you that? You thought so much and so well that you always inserted the citations in the right places. You didn't need to swallow them and then disgorge them as if they were your own pearls. But you turned into an oyster—a mollusk, less of a person.

At first, I'd get offended, lash back—I'd make a scene. But then I'd stop myself—you never made scenes. "What difference does it make?" I'd say instead. "You aren't seriously throwing a fit because I forgot a story came from you."

Lia was like that. The party structure was like that: a club where the person who managed to hunt down and consume other people's qualities the fastest got ahead. And that, you used to explain, wasn't lying. You'd entered a specialized world where omission didn't count as lying. And betrayal counted only when it was repeated many times, in the same places, with the same people. Everything else—indiscretions, sex, conspiracy, complaints—was just human antics.

Your moral code became bureaucratic; there were subheadings for every infraction. And even the biggest ones ceased to matter much. You learned that there's not much distance between a slipup and a crime. That all of us are capable, at any point, of sliding into darkness. One drink, two, a drunk, a murderer; a joint, a line of coke, an addiction, a thief. That's how life was. Unfamiliar. At once enormously simple and enormously complex. Music growing ever louder, until it was deafening. Without any truth as a starting point.

"What difference does it make? It's way worse when those guys steal one of my projects and take credit for it. And I've gotten used to that—they're men, there are a lot of them, that's how they've always run things. War is fought with missiles, so it's no use wearing yourself out hurling rocks."

You had an answer for everything, damn you. Back when you were studying history, you'd specialized in questions. You interrogated the past, earnestly, methodically: Why was this like that? Why didn't the other possibilities come to pass? Where was the truth, regardless of the facts?

People used to laugh when you talked about truth. They'd insist there was no such thing; that's what passed for truth in the splinter of time we happened to inhabit. But you never settled into our time. And you were always worrying about settling into some other time, turning into an anachronism.

"I don't care if they think I'm old-fashioned. But it bugs me to think that my ideas might just be reactions, rather than a self-sufficient philosophy. We can't let ourselves drift into enemy territory, darling."

Enemy territory. You could sketch it out with the clarity of a soccer match. You liked soccer because it resembled the truth. Even when the referees were corrupt and banknotes flowed in greasy rivers under the tables of accountants, businessmen, lawyers. Even when it turned into a business. Good and bad, pure and impure—yes, the flow of cash did make it harder to draw such distinctions. But the sun on the field determined everything—men's legs racing after the ball of truth.

"It's so clear which players are giving everything they've got and which are just using their bodies," you'd say. "Why isn't life as transparent as soccer?"

3

Whose death is this, laid out in a coffin? Where does it come from, this icy fever sealing my mouth? I struggle to escape this box where they've put me on display to be mourned. If only they knew how to pray. Our Father, I no longer want to go to heaven. The smell of the dead unsettles the living, so they smother it with flowers, incense, candles, anything to keep that smell far from the actual body, still flesh, still warm. In the dead person's place is a dazed, dizzying fear. Fear of me, of the future that I, in my burial garb, portend. That fear creates waves of heat, somber waves that expand in the candlelight, the slavering whispers.

Are you afraid of me too? I lie motionless here, my eyes closed, looking at you to avoid looking at myself, to forget the smell of fear that may be the final scent. I concentrate on you, on the smell of the beach, seaweed and rocks, the smell of the sea we used to plunge into together, the smells of life that rescue me from this dense fog, from this swell of irremediable pity. Our Father, let me look at him. Let my dead eyes rise on the candlelight, slowly, to look at him.

Finally, I see you. I never dreamed I'd see you in mismatched socks—one gray, the other black. I noticed when you crossed your legs and straightened your spine with a sigh, lolling your head back, and only then did I feel a pang. Because that suffering pose of yours, sitting for an hour with your chin lowered, might not have meant anything. Or, rather, it might have meant so many things that it became a blank, with a somber elegance that remained immensely remote from me.

I spent my whole life trying to interpret you—what a delightful waste! It wasn't even out of love. At least, not that phenomenon that pushes people to an exalted state of possessiveness and lust. Through you, I existed before I was even born, in the harsh, secret vocabulary of a war that no longer belonged to me: no can do, bullshit, whatever. We never felt vertigo, not even momentarily, not even that night we chugged your prized bottle of aged Irish whiskey and stayed up to watch the sun rise over Lisbon's rooftops. In a way, we knew each other's bodies by heart; we swapped inhibitions and gaffes the way kids swap trading cards. It wasn't just happiness; it was a kind of astonished pride in our exchange of dismal intimacies. Without sleeping with you, I learned from you about a man's triumphs and tribulations, the turbulent brutality of pleasure, the terror of failure, the multiplicity of surrenders as a rule of absolute surrender.

Most of all, I liked watching you. Selecting Italian silk scarves, for example, opening and closing the drawers organized by color. You could have lived off bread, water, and cigarettes, but you never left the house without a pure silk scarf around your neck. I found your scarves so embarrassing at first, wrote you off as profligate because of them. I was the opposite: appalled that it was possible to spend a month's salary on a scrap of cloth. I bought my clothing out of baskets at the market in colors reminiscent of 1950s movies, left it heaped on the back of the chair in my room for weeks on end. But you liked looking at me. You liked my white sneakers amid all those high heels, the circle of my pink skirts among the navy-blue suits. I was always what I seemed, and you were everything you seemed. I think that's why we were so close—and why we pulled so far apart.

When, in a flicker of candles, your face appeared above mine, I hadn't seen you for almost a year. With what you used to call my naughty sense of humor—and here I'll pause to confirm that, yes, it's the last thing to go—I felt like laughing at your woebegone demeanor. Had I been able to, obviously. What were you pondering there, with a widower's eloquent composure? A list of your girlfriends? The theme for your next party? A trip to New York? And then you crossed your legs. You remained sitting with them crossed for a good half hour and never noticed your terrible blunder. Nobody was relaxed, not you or anybody else—the light at a wake is dim, and the deceased, despite our efforts, are too present. Now I was the deceased. I'm still so unaccustomed to it that the word deceased doesn't fit. That's why I'm seeking you with words of life, the words with which

16

you recognized me and loved me. But what do I know of the hours you spent at my wake, what do I know of time, now that life is unspooling before me like a far-off film?

In this place without place, past present and future are simultaneous. They tumble into the depths of their own overabundant existence. But the ache persists, glows amid the chaos. My eyes that are no longer mine now see all that was, all that could be, all that is. I focus on what is—I'm dead, everyone's crying over me, stripped of the trite, continual, mineral malice that the living wield as a law of survival. This was the glory I dreamed of as a teenager: to gather everybody's sadness and longing around my own absence.

Everybody's? I'm missing somebody who is not you. I'm missing the place of my own death—the darkness of a staircase where you can hear the rain falling, a staircase where I learned to cry. I was that place, the antechamber of passion. I was the inside of a man who can't bear to see me dead. At the moment, he's lying on the floor in the place where he killed me many years ago. I know he's there, in that now-abandoned house, that house he kept for himself. That house I loved, still love, which he kept for me. I lean against the door of the cockeyed house that contains everything you don't know about me, all that I never wanted to know and was. I can never knock on that door again, never cry so the door will open and show me, through the blur of my tears, the place of love. I'm dead. Everybody's crying over me. He's crying. There's no rain, just the sound of his tears. There was never any rain, only our tears, the tears I am once more fleeing for the glimmering lap of our immanent, moribund, immortal friendship. Don't let me go to heaven, darling. I was always so scared you were right. What if heaven is the disillusionment that serves as the cornerstone of your beliefs? What if our misspent friendship is out of place in the perfection of heaven? Let me be your life's throbbing beauty, to the extent that life can actually be yours.

3

I was in a funk when I met you. One of the few periods like that in my life. My second divorce, retirement, the death of a close friend. I wallowed in the easy enumeration of those reasons. But getting divorced had been my idea, and I'd requested early retirement because I was sick of the bank. Only Alexandre's death went against my own desires. Suddenly, I was almost old—like I'd wanted to be all my life. With the right to grumble, to be pompous and irascible, to have my ideas respected, just like anyone who has nothing more to hope for from life. And I found myself hollowed out, without knowing why. Wanting to complain for no reason, to pontificate senselessly. To experience once more the afflicted arrogance of youth. I signed up for the history class to fill that hole. I needed the blood of endless battle. I needed the blood of other people's ideas, the blood of the history of the future that flows through university classrooms, through the turbulent margins of books. I've been fascinated by history since I was a boy. It seemed like a good time to cultivate that old interest. And it was also a way of paying posthumous homage to my mother, who'd always lamented that I never pursued higher education.

I didn't hear a word you said the whole first class; I was hypnotized, so to speak, by your extraordinary sweater. Electric-blue wool with sailboats and dolphins. You looked about fifteen years old—and that's not a compliment. I couldn't believe a high school girl from the suburbs had anything to teach me. In the following weeks, I amused myself by turning your youthful buzzing into words. You drove me crazy. According to you, the entire history of civilization was built on the systematic objective of discriminating against women. Lou Salomé, as it turned out, was the author of Rilke's poems and Freud's psychoanalysis; Alma Mahler had composed her husband's symphonies; Camille Claudel was the spirit of Rodin's sculptures; and so on. You were pissed when I said the course should be renamed History of Muses instead of Great Thinkers of the Western Tradition. Far from being cowed, you assigned me an extra paper on muses' influence on the Great Thinkers. In it, I argued that muses functioned merely as a mirror that amplified the creator's light. You gave me a 9 out of 10 and decided to ignore me. This game brought color back into my life. I came out of my blue period and entered one that was ruby-colored, which hadn't happened to me since the glory days of the revolution. I started reading stacks of books, collecting arguments I could use to crush you. But I also enjoyed discovering the constellation of women you were introducing me to. I became smitten with the black eyebrows—so similar to your own—of Frida Kahlo. Her glorious, raw self-portraits. You remained immune to my attempts at charm. To tell the truth, I wasn't used to women resisting the natural magnetism of my blue eyes. My good looks, which had brought so much trouble into my life, left you cold—you, a girl of modest physical attributes, wearing a sailboats-and-dolphins sweater and spouting theories about liberation. And that intrigued me.

4

There are so many things I never told you—and you used to say I talked too much. I float through this nolus in search of those missing words, which stretch between us like the long corridor of a prison. When I was alive, I used to say I couldn't forgive you for how much you didn't know about me. Here in this nolus, I now see the unassailable truth: I can't forgive myself for how much I was unable to pour into you. You should have been my heir, the prolongation of my light. At midnight, as 1990 turned over into a new year, we paused our game of mah-jongg and you hugged me tight. "If I'm not here in the year 2000," you murmured, "you play for me. And do me a favor and win for a change, kid." Neither of us considered the alternate possibility—you were fifty-three at the time, and I was just twenty-eight. I thought I wanted to change the world; I thought you just wanted a change of scenery. I thought I was thinking—that's why I learned so little about unthinkable us. Faith can become a sort of arrogance, and you knew it, though you were always tactful enough not to tell me. You used coarseness as a scalpel, going after the tumors in my understanding and excising them with swift brutality so I wouldn't get tangled up. But you never came close to my central nervous system.

You might tell me, "You think you're better than other people because you're protected by a God they do not know." It was absolutely true, but my own past wouldn't have allowed me to recognize it. And then you'd laugh and fall silent. I'd say barbaric things, like "I want to change the world; you just want a change of scenery," and your face would dim, fall, and your mouth would let out a harsh guffaw; and you'd say, "Amen." I nestled inside my noble conscience—mirror, mirror on the wall, who's got the purest sentiments of all?

Don't cry for me, darling: the best of me lives on in you—it will always be alive in that knowledge of fragmentation I lacked, in that courage of incompleteness I can see only now, at last, from this nolus. I was your professor at the university; I was never able to be your mentor, but I found in you a privilege greater than that of teaching: a soul that added color to the canvas I provided. "Your Jesus is the militant revolutionary who drove the money changers out of the temple," you once told me, when I first got into politics. "That sort of God, the tempestuous kind, draws crowds and amplifies the power of sacred texts. As a teacher, though, you were more like the Jesus who forgave Judas, the one who graced Judas with that ladder of love we call forgiveness. That Jesus was just a man capable of unforgivable things, one in solidarity with human weakness. That's the only Jesus I'm interested in."

I thought you were saying it out of envy, you know. In small countries, envy takes on a huge, mystifying quality, and conspiracy theories bloom in the flower beds of our impatience. Lacking ingenuity and skill, we barricade ourselves in impatient theories. My transition from teaching to politics was always a theoretical insubordination—and I thought I was fleeing from theory toward the greater art of living.

What is it I taught you, in the end? Everything original in my doctoral dissertation was written and thought by you. Instead of encouraging you to pursue an academic career, I cheated off you, copied your essays on the paradoxes of feminist ideals, won praise at the expense of your anonymous creativity. And I convinced myself that it had all been just the opposite, that I was the one who'd put the ideas in your head that you then returned to me, slightly expanded. I was, by definition, perfect, chosen by God. If I'd at least just said thank you. God of my imperfection, pour a dram of my dead voice into my friend's dreams; let me give him the thanks I so badly owe.

4

And to think I used to say you talked too much. It's true you never stopped talking. Even or especially without words, with the movement of your body, the force of your hugs. I didn't know how to hug like you—sometimes I'd shake you, just out of distress—you know, fits of shyness that set my molecules boiling. The hug you gave me that New Year's Eve, a decade ago now—did I know how to receive it? Did I ever hug you the way you deserved?

When you were alive, I could believe in souls, moles, intergalactic bowls—whatever you wanted. Because people looked at you and saw something transparent and solid, that knot of blood, secretions, and light pulsing like a beacon. Now, everything and everybody talks about "the spirit that remains." Your parents invoke you, you and dozens of other residents of Paradise, as a way of moving on—church masses are supposed to be quick, efficient, by the book. But I can't quite believe in abstract souls, discreet air bubbles belched up between a cup of tea and two sighs.

I miss you, damn it—have I said that already? Why doesn't your seraphic Jesus come to succor me? Why won't he bring you back to life—just for a few hours, Lord; what's a few measly hours for a guy who's basking in eternity?

Oh, kid. The world sorely misses your absolute certainties about good and evil. Even if they were pretty simplistic and full of holes.

Your soul always had a bit of a limp, muddy pant cuffs, a hastily packed suitcase, the rumpled clothing of the inveterate traveler. But it limped so gracefully, honey. You swiped some of my papers on sublime womanhood—and I thoroughly enjoyed how tormented you were by that shameless act. I never accused you, never teased you about it—not even once. To make you suffer, I confess, to show you I'd noticed. Oh, puerile, pathetic stratagems.

How I wish I could give you now the vast, childlike love I had for you. I rationed it my whole life like a goddamn candy bar. Why do we live as if we had infinite amounts of time, as if we could do it all over again, as if we could do anything at all? I hope you haven't carried that foolish guilt with you in death. I hope you know I was proud of you, puffed up and preening when you incorporated my lowly essays into your dissertation. If it weren't for you, I never would have studied all those warrior women—and now that nobody's listening, I'll admit that your heroines helped enliven my existence. No question.

Omnipotent God I don't believe in, wake from your eternal slumber and go give my friend the thanks I was never able to whisper in her ear. Don't pretend not to hear me, cruel, lazy God. Watch out, I could destroy you. And I'll do it, but first I'll destroy your fame and glory. Or do you think I've forgotten the hell you rained down on me in Africa? If I survived that, hard-hearted God, I'll survive you too.

5

I wish I could stop seeing you. You've started growing a beard again, like the one you had when we met. It never suited you. You loll in bed for hours in the mornings, listening to the songs I used to love and you despised— "That's not music, man, it's a way for soulless losers to pass the time." You never listen to your classical music, the great operas sung by the great vocalists, the great symphonies by the great maestros. I used music as a soundtrack, songs made to the measure of every mood: Chico Buarque, Joni Mitchell, Sérgio Godinho, Serge Gainsbourg, and even—to your immense horror—the fados of Amália Rodrigues, which only reminded you of the dreary country into which I'd not yet been born, the misery of the war that crushed your idealism.

Please stop. Being here, so far away, so far from my hand on your head, I can't stand hearing that song of Pascoal's: "I want the dark light of contagious dreams / The scraps of the souls we invented / The burning heart of old flames / The stories we never ended up telling." I first heard it ages ago, back when the song was new and I was in love with an astrophysicist I didn't marry only because he couldn't bear Portugal's mediocrity and I couldn't stand the idea of living far from Lisbon, however mediocre it was.

We were very young; we knew everything. To us, life was a multimedia in-stallation created by our hands for our own glory. We believed we all had our own paths. And look at me now. You can't see me, of course; most likely you're already forgetting the color of my skin, my faded scars. I'm close to you, hovering above the roof of your house, beneath the airplanes' dreamlike trails, in these wispy clouds that offer a narrow view of everything. I can see you, your neighbors, your street. I can choose whatever streets I want—they're all identical now that I'm not in them. The city's streets served as our mirror, remember? Uneven sidewalks, unspooling hills offering a bonus glimpse of river blue, battered tiles from other lives, avenues that suddenly expanded but somehow remained lackluster. My steps make no echo; my voice casts no shadow. It's you I see because I can't stop thinking about you. I want to unwrap the Great Mystery: What's your life like now, so far from me? I find you living the way I used to live—except for that Pascoal song. You weren't around the first time I heard it. I was holding hands with the young astrophysicist who should have married me. Pascoal was singing almost in a whisper, accompanied by just a viola. He was rehearsing, making sure the song was perfect. He used to invite a few friends to secret pre-shows sometimes, where he would appear with a birdlike, almost timid nervousness, as if he, too, were very young and everything might be immensely important. You weren't around then, but later, when you were, I used to sing that song to you as you walked me home at dawn. We'd stroll through the city at that hour when the sunlight mingles with the yellow cinders of the streetlamps. We'd breathe in the clean air of those early hours, a damp air that made the streetcar tracks glisten and soaked the lowered shades to a dusty pink. You were afraid of the dark. That's why you used to lie down in the morning, while I often didn't even do that—I'd take a shower and head out into the world. Now I can't sleep anymore—I watch over your slumber without knowing whom to watch over. You fall asleep to the sound of my songs—after Pascoal, then Brel, Aznavour and his Venice of dead loves, light songs, little ditties to touch housekeepers' emotions, you used to say, ditties that now slake your secret housekeeper heart and shout that there's no longer anything I can do for you, for me, for all those hours we forgot to live.

5

How many days will it take me to forget your face? I remember you constantly. Detail by detail, so as not to lose you. So as to lose myself, all of me, in the mutable object that was you. Your deep-black eyes, perpetually dark-circled. Those Kahlo eyebrows. The aquiline nose that made you self-consciously avoid showing your profile in photos. The birthmark on the right side of your neck. Your long, bony arms. Your hands, square like your fingernails, which were always clipped short. No polish. A matter of principle: nail polish was just another blatant symbol of women's subjugation, or worse, because of the time it took. I agreed with your aversion, but for aesthetic reasons: for me, sharp, brightly colored claws evoked barbaric customs, shantytown odors, primitive rituals. The grace of your pointy elbows resting on the table, your hands shredding the night faster than your words. Your wide mouth, with its row of large, uneven teeth, always poised for your next laugh.

You once tracked me down at an art opening, your eyes swimming with tears because some marquise or other upper-crust dame had told you, with a beneficent smile, that she knew a great dentist and recommended that you go get your teeth fixed. You retorted, apparently, that your teeth were just fine, that their crookedness was part of your unique charm, to which the marquise responded, sneering in C minor, how marvelous it was that some people are happy the way they are. You told me all this in a rush, whispering in my ear in a tremulous voice, and I was furious. I gave you my arm, and we marched over to the woman, whereupon I looked her scornfully up and down and said, "Don't take this the wrong way, but there are treatments nowadays for those ugly age spots on your hands. I'd be happy to give you the name of a great dermatologist. She's really a miracle worker."

I didn't just do it for you, kid. I took a wicked pleasure in cutting such people down to size; their swift transit from surprise to horror disfigured them, revealing their scaly, interplanetary crocodile heads. We became experts at that game of truth-telling, drawing inspiration from John Carpenter's *They Live*, one of the many movies we went to see together.

Initially, you declared it a lesser work, entertaining but crude. As you sank into the mire of politics, though, you came to see it as a documentary. They really do live, and it's only with special sunglasses that some of us are able to see them. Others, like you, fight to eliminate them so the world can be the humane place it hasn't yet become. The problem, my dear, is that those who fight the hardest seem doomed to burn themselves out.

Your God's lightning, if he exists, is much more of a threat than the two of us put together. Since you kicked the bucket, all I see are crocodiles. And you're right: they wear Hugo Boss suits, Ralph Lauren shirts. Even, I'm forced to admit, Italian silk scarves like mine. Identification by accessory, you used to joke. Like in primitive communities. But aren't we all, even those of us who know, tribal beings governed by the principle of participation? What logic is there in this chaotic discourse that binds me to you, that makes me look for you in the cruel green of this false spring?

I don't believe in gods or devils. And yet I receive your signals, locked in solitude and listening for you. There you are: "I want the dark light of contagious dreams / The scraps of the souls we invented

/ The burning heart of old flames / The stories we never ended up telling." The voice of your friend Pascoal, one of the lucky guys you fell in love with before me.

Yesterday I had the distinct impression you were asking me to play a bunch of those songs you used to love so that you could listen to them. It's weird, but I obeyed—even though I despise that crap. You used to say that if music were a great art, there'd be a panoply of female composers. But there's not a single woman among the greats. What's more, dictators are all music lovers. For you, this was irrefutable proof that music was a trivial, everyday kind of art. Strangely, if you'll forgive the observation, your own favorite singers were almost all men, my dear. Worse than that, even: sensitive men.

6

If only I could occupy you without the strangeness of pain, wake up again inside your head, so deep inside my own that you don't even sense I might be about to disappear. It was Pascoal who introduced you to me. Pascoal, whose life is half melodies and half cries of pain; Pascoal, the doctor who traded salvation for emotion and who falls asleep every night with at least one dead soul burdening his dreams. He wanted to save me, I wouldn't let him, and now he's swamped with regret—survival's persistent prize. You keep insisting things like, "There wasn't anything you could do, forget about it."

You're the only one who can't forget me. Do we ever forget a part of who we are? We forget only what we can isolate in our memory—and for a long time now, you haven't even been remembering me. If I look at your present self, I find you wallowing in the hangover of our friendship, talking about my overweening ambition or my cheesy tastes with some distant acquaintance. Or letting them do it, which is the same thing. That's why I can't look away from what we were, both together and apart. Trying to wipe the heavens clean of the cruel words I also said or let be said about you. So many words, so pathetic in their tattered cloaks of cowardice.

I carry you in our stifled laughter, the tears you wept over me, a fire escape to the wisdom of happiness, in skin scalded by the night's glow after hours at the beach. We've talked too much for me to remember what we talked about, lived too many lives for me to be able to separate them. To be able to separate myself from you. Memory tends to unravel like old viscera in this space I will call merely incorporeal so as not to frighten you. I see everything, continuously; the spectacle of life interferes with the routes of my wanderings into the past. But what is the past? Only for the living do the dead have a past—the worst thing about death is this obligatory present, this suspended nolus.

In this obligatory present, I see my mother: tired, not just of my father but also of me, sobbing with rage on the telephone for having fallen into the trap of becoming pregnant and getting married. And for the first time, I doubt this God who refuses me the mercy of altering the images of the past. Or at least blocking my access to them. One day I'll look at you, and I won't even know who we were. Understandings, misunderstandings, rage, resentment—everything becomes a dull, heavy mass that I'll gradually leave behind.

I start seeing you outside of time, strain to review what brought me here, hanging practically over your shoulder. I'd like to be able to stroke your long gray hair, touch your slender hands, hug you—all those things we used to think were so corny. I lean over your head, but I can't decipher your thoughts—remember Wenders's angels, hunched by the powerlessness of omniscience? The state I find myself in is even more excruciating: as if I were drowsily watching a movie I can no longer re-create, seeing it all, the past and the future, which ultimately are a single hermaphroditic creature, and learning too late what I was unable to see. This must be limbo.

God will come looking for me—or, more humbly, will send someone else to look for me—to lead me to another dimension. Will you come? Are you so human, God of my faith, that you seek people's love only to forget them? If so, maybe I deserve to be appointed your guardian angel. It would be a divine bit of vengeance, my friend. Or, seriously speaking, it would be a restoration of the justice of things. And especially of peace—the peace that won so little of our respect.

That photo of me on the bedside table in your bedroom—was it already there, or did you pull it out when you heard I'd died? They matter so little, these pinpricks of emotions. Slow childhood cruelties. My mother's shrieking eyes when she caught me dissecting silkworms. I just wanted to see what they were made of. How that spongy thing turned into a butterfly. I wanted to see what stuff your love for me was made of. I needed to compress your heart to fit it inside mine.

And now I have to take it out again so I can leave this limbo. But I don't know how. Without your heart, I'm unable to love—don't abandon me again. And to think I used to love everybody. Loving in the abstract is much more agile than loving concretely.

It's clear now that my dedication to Important Causes grew in inverse proportion to my disappointment with the Important People in my life. I thought of friendship as a grown-up, sanitized version of love, so I transferred the heavy artillery of my affections to its armory. I swapped out Prince Charming for Friend Wonderful, which was you. You could have been my father; you were my disciple. Nothing could tear us apart: we were naturally free of the pitfalls of desire, the via crucis of possession and sacrifice. So naïve. An entire life wasted being naïve—and I didn't even have time to change the world.

God is merciful; he's put me here with you instead of sending my soul to one of those countries where mothers mutilate their own daughters, slicing their genitals with a knife and stitching them up with thorns. I hear those girls' screams constantly—they woke me up my whole life. I'd open my eyes hearing those screams issuing from Somalia or Sudan, those screams that could have been mine. I thought I possessed all the keys to suffering. You used to call me presumptuous, and maybe you were right. There's no such thing as a true understanding of another's suffering—only that paternalistic distance known, in fortunate cases, as compassion. And that can be enough as a guerrilla tactic, but not as a theory of triumph. And without the sere blood of theory, the grace of Possible Paradise remains out of reach. Without theory, I, the everyday infiltration of your soul, do not exist.

I always lived in theory, afraid of the black voids between flashes—much more so than you. And that's how we are still—I, the daughter of a slovenly God, and you, a fervent devotee of unthinkable distances. I can't think without you. I slip through the spongy walls of death and find you orphaned—you can't love without me.

We were made for each other. We coincided even as we rejected coincidence, with the peevishness typical of the impoverished, confined in the prison of their penury. We were made for each other and never figured it out, choosing instead to respect the protocols of our time, to prioritize the urgent voice of the body. We were made for each other another way—a way that was dark, dense, transcendent. What could we, slaves to the Supreme Intelligence, know of transcendence? How could we, illustrious servants of history, grasp the tremulous light of the small miracle granted to us? Every morning I leaped from the sheets like a flame. I was going to eradicate human brutality. I was going to do away with the banality of evil. And I was going to do away, truth be told, with my own painful anonymity. I left the earth without ever getting it any closer to being free of savagery, but my God faults me only for the inadequacy of my love for you.

Immortality is irrelevant. From this side of death, it's mortality that shines: knowing that I was mortal gave mass and color to the stones that paved my path; because I was mortal, the moon reminded me of love and mystery, and my desire to persist into the future trembled in the star-flooded sky. Mortality, which only human beings know, is the only incomprehensible substance there is. The dizzying disorientation of mortality led me to teaching: groups of eager-eyed youths arrayed before me in a succession reminiscent of wispy clouds on a summer night. Until you appeared, with your assortment of ages all rolled into one, and restored my nearly depleted youth.

6

There's a sort of ethical energy at funerals. A desire for goodness that flings stardust in people's eyes and snuffs out little everyday resentments. Tomorrow we'll go back to envying one another. Bad-mouthing our neighbors behind their backs. Betraying close friends in business meetings. Being nice only once in a while. But tomorrow you won't be here to cry out that it's the once-in-a-while that matters. You won't be here to wipe the dust off humanity and make those souls shine again. What is a soul—can you tell me that? You used to toss your head back and intone theatrically, authentically, "The soul is a vice." "Those aren't your words, they're Fanny Owen's in Dona Agustina's novel," I'd remind you. You'd shrug and laugh: "Sure, but that sentence changed my life. And the things that transform us belong to us, you jerk, whether you like it or not." And then, to annoy you, I'd decline that noun in the key of north flat: "The soul is a slice, the soul is a price, the soul is fried rice . . ." You'd run your fingers through your hair and sigh: "All that too, yes, even if you don't dare acknowledge it." Did you once tell me I was the echo of your soul, or am I making things up now?

When things stop, they change. The simple fact of ceasing to be changes them, however much we try to make them stay the same. I'd love to have tapes of our conversations, movies of the walks we took. But when I watched the recording later, I'd be somebody else.

Somebody else pondering an image that was no longer me, that was no longer you, only an aura—the aura that films manufacture, light cast by what no longer is, by what we now never were, even if we once had been. The final montage of *Annie Hall* that you loved as if it were your own life—and it was your life, the fervent, chaotic life you dreamed of at fourteen; the avid, energetic life you built like a castle from scattered LEGOs. That montage was at once the apotheosis and the negation of the film itself, because the only love that endures is that of dark apotheoses, a love that can't stand montages. Silly girl. Go on and laugh at me now, a castaway from you, adrift on my own brain. It's got woodworm, my brain does, and nothing sticks. Pascoal gives me a long hug and apologizes for not having hurdled the barrier of your aloofness to save you. I tell him, "There wasn't anything you could do, forget about it."

And I'm angry at myself. So angry that I get angry at him in order to survive. We do so many stupid things to survive—if you only knew. You didn't want to know; you wanted to see the firefighters who save people, the Mandelas who resist, the young military officers who hand us carnation-shaped freedom and then head home. Where others counted knife wounds, you'd tally up kind gestures. Ever sensible, you were wary of heroes who were propped up by the press or swathed in exotic robes. Not even in the ferment of adolescence did you get swept up in romanticized views of terrorists designed to supplant Russian chauffeurs in the hearts of thrill-seeking rich girls. You always had a gift for seeing things clearly, that rare gift known, with a disdain proportional to its rarity, as common sense.

And so, nonsensically, I direct my anger toward the gentle eyes of your friend who had a premonition and could not save you. If he'd just called me, damn it. I'd have gone looking for you—but no, I wouldn't have, because I never believed in premonitions. Still don't—they're always in hindsight, calling attention to the enlightened party after the misfortune has already taken place. I don't believe in anything, actually, except what you used to call "goodness" and I, allergic to the whiff of churchiness that abstract nouns give off, preferred to call "the possibility of human renewal."

Yes, we shared a view of the world that scornful cynics find overly optimistic. For every act of horror, we found infinite acts of love. Our shared passion for history led us to human generosity: in the shadow of every dictator, we found a throng of democrats; in the creases of each massacre, thousands of lives devoted to other people's happiness. The sowers of horror were always a minority—an effective minority, sure, but one that grows in exact proportion to people's belief in their power. And the two of us refused to believe. That persistent refusal was, for us, a war against the propagandistic expansion of terror. You saw Christ in everybody, while I simply saw the person in everybody. Which was exactly the same thing, apart from your prayers and my conviction that bloodshed is sometimes necessary.

Are you praying for me now? "Angel of God, my guardian dear, to whom God's love commits me here . . ." Is it possible? Even though you know I'd happily wring your God's neck if it would bring you back to life. Is it possible? Live by the sword, die by the sword. You reap what you sow. Is it possible? Are you catching my drift here, in the jungle tongue of the vox populi you loved so much?

You're just a photo beside my insomnia now. A memory that, like all memories, is mostly about what never existed. With this photograph, I am forgetting you. Meticulously, every time I strive to retain you, and so I am beginning to invent you. Everything in you has wings now—your laughter, your footsteps. Even the few sentences of yours that I recall contain a rustling of feathers. And I slip into this too-human loneliness of not knowing how to be alone again, the way I was when you still existed, in this very city, and I didn't even think about you anymore.

7

It's three thirty in the morning, according to your clock. On this August night, you're sitting in front of the TV watching the latest Rolling Stones concert. One day, to your great horror, I compared the Stones' music to Vergílio Ferreira's books: they'd both dedicated their whole lives to exacerbating the ache of adolescence. In his late fifties, Mick Jagger maintains the posture, the energy, the frenetic movement of an uninhibited teenager. It is what it was, but even more so— and that image-driven discipline, rather than being pathetic, produces a curious model of rigor and integrity. The other Stones look like old birds wrapped in peacock feathers—but in young people they inspired the notion of rebellious old age. Mick was pure fury, sex and innocence in cold combustion—and he still is.

You were pre-Stones, and you laughed. You told me my obsession with that group of ill-mannered men only revealed my youth. You were right, and that's why the Rolling Stones still exist: because they feed on the most fleeting of all mortalities and reproduce it, gesture by gesture, unto exhaustion. Like Vergílio's writing—singing and re-creating the voracious persistence of beauty, dismantling ugliness's erotic core.

Of course there's an unquenchable desert of differences between all things— but why did you insist on focusing on that desert instead of seeking communion with works of art? I was annoyed by your erudition—life, for you, was a museum of contrasts. And look at you now, seduced by the Mick Jagger of eternal youth, seduced by me, in the foggy mirror of time. The shadow that I am falls over your body, and we shine, a blue glow in the cold of your dawn.

7

In the dark living room, the TV is giving off a blue haze that seems to pull you inside. This rush of moving melancholy summons you. Inside the screen, Mick Jagger is leaping around. A man who doesn't even know you existed, who maybe doesn't even exist himself beyond this stereophonic image that reminds me of you. "I wanted to see his real eyes and mouth and face, but they weren't there. They were a diffuse, ineluctable apparition, like the light of the air that can't be seen and is merely illumination." Your voice saying those words. What book did you read them in?

You had a habit of repeating aloud the sentences you found most striking, regardless of how silently other people might be reading other things. I'd muster my best fake smile, saying, "That's nice, really nice." And then you'd get excited and rattle out an entire chapter. It was incredibly irritating, in the moment—I was trying to read something else. But later, after you'd left, back when it was possible for you to leave, I'd remember your reading, the husky solemnity of your voice, and I'd smile, staggered by that sudden sweet memory of you.

8

I need your life to be infected with the flesh of my death. I need you to be me—
not like a son or daughter, no, much more than that. A child is another hypothesis of life—in the best hypothesis, a child is all that we were not. They leave us
detritus—blind anguish, impatience, modeling-resistant clay, what we didn't
want to be. We end up loving them wildly to avoid confronting the lack of love
from which they are born—our hidden darkness, formed of dead passions and
endless frustrations.

 I've met a lot of children produced in the fever of reconciliation, conceived in memoriam to yesteryear's happiness. Others marked the precise apex
of passion—the moment of splendor that precedes death. All children are born
posthumous to a love that no longer floats in the air they breathe. Attempts,
temptations to increase the knowledge of life, when life is known only through
the shadowy door of ignorance, of misunderstanding. Of the asymmetrical energies that have made possible that thing we call humanity—detritus of detritus, born of the disequilibrium of matter.

 You used to say my imagination was absurdly combative; I'd retort, unfairly,
that I'd rather it be absurdly combative than resignedly hierarchical, like yours.
I was fascinated by Chew and Mandelstam's theory that explained the grad-
ual transformation of the universe via the collision of particles of equal value,
and I tried to assess history using that notion of a world of pure differences in
confrontation.

8

I organized my existence around infatuations. As a result, all love and all victories were permitted to me: I was already dead. I strangled love affairs in the cradle, which had the advantage of making them incandescent—and the disadvantage of making them sterile. No woman offers a child to a man who honestly admits he cannot be relied on. At bottom, that's what the famous maternal instinct is all about: blood offerings to provoke commitment and guilt in men. When the plan falls through, the human jewel is transformed into a simulacrum of the beloved object—and the child serves as a glorious abandonment of life.

I once told one woman, "I don't think I can grow old with you, but I'd like to have a child with you before we break up." It was a huge declaration of love, but my lover was unmoved by my sincerity; she packed her bags and took off the next day. That saintly woman had tried for three years to convert me to conjugality. She'd accidentally leave her shampoo in my bathtub. I'd return it to her, smiling broadly, the next time we saw each other. She'd ask permission to leave a spare shirt in my wardrobe. She once told me, "I know that deep down you truly need my love." I replied with the easy stereotypes of your professorial discourse—and I hadn't even met you yet: "Deep-down men are a fantasy that women came up with so they can keep being victims without undermining the advances of contemporary society."

And so I ended up an involuntary orphan of the child I never had. And I never knew what it would be like to love somebody beyond the brief flame of infatuation. And you, you scamp—I'd almost forgotten about you when you up and died on me.

And here I am, trapped by the dark memory of your eyes, your leaping footsteps, your stubborn joy that eventually began to make my life too sweet. I can't focus. I spend my days staring at the words in the books I'm supposed to be reading and can't manage to process them. And over and over I listen to Pascoal's song: "The shadow of the clouds on the sea / The wind dancing in the rain / A steaming cup of tea / Everything spoke to me of you / The shadow of the clouds has dropped / The wide sky has cooled / And the wild sea has lost / Its light that came from you." How long has it been since my heart burned?

9

I was always the nostalgic type, especially regarding things that never came to pass. The marvels still to come. You must concentrate on happiness so I can continue to exist there in it with you. You differed from most members of your generation in your love of novelty. History is a school of optimism—despite everything. Fernando Savater used to say he'd have refused to be born prior to the invention of anesthesia, remember?

The two of us took great pleasure in confirming the ways the world had improved—isn't life today infinitely more agreeable than during slavery, the Inquisition, or Nazism? Others would argue that slaves, inquisitors, and Nazis, victims and torturers, still exist. But we'd respond, insistent, with this simple truth: they exist, but we're aware of it. And we're aware of it because we no longer participate in such savagery. We're domesticated now—we created laws and rights and strove to make them universal.

When we looked around, we didn't see the much-bemoaned erosion of values, except in those who denounced it most vehemently. In our view, the great void lay in consensus stereotypes about a mythical past, Before the Soul's Fall. As if souls plunged into the water in choreographed simultaneity, dunking their flower wreaths and long legs in Esther Williams–style illuminated tanks. As if the soul were not a vice, and therefore durable, a thing that even the pale Fanny Owen could, in classic Dona Agustina fashion, unveil. As if "the void" had not been, since time immemorial, what panicked people have called the blossoming of the new, now returned anew.

So there's an international network of Hawkers of Dead Values—High Authorities of this and that. They get cars, offices, and sky-high salaries for dictating the limits of morality. Their thinking coincides with that of those who pay them, yet they consider themselves genuinely innocent and free. But in what other era of history was there so much talk of ethics? What other era saw the establishment of so many organizations working to defend children, the disabled, women, animals, prisoners, people on death row? The philosophy of decline, so in vogue, seemed to us merely the democratic version of the philosophy of dictatorship. A way of pruning creative intelligence: take shelter, my children, the world is ending.

Not a day goes by, in these years at millennium's end, that one of these Great Creators doesn't declare, standing before a euphoria of cameras and an eager audience, that literature, cinema, theater, or painting is at death's door. I see them solemnly captaining the epic shipwreck of their enlightened posterities. I slip into the steamy air of a café in late afternoon and encounter a woman of about forty-five, sapped by the endless effort to appear no more than twenty-five, who lights a cigarette and says, "Oh, young people these days don't fall in love the way we used to." Twenty years before her, another woman of about forty-five, much older looking because surgery hadn't yet made such strides, will have said, "Oh, we used to fall in love much deeper than these young people today."

The two of us never talked like that: Oh, back in our day; oh, young people. We never let ourselves get suckered into a retouched version of that ancient ideology that mistakes transformation for degeneration. I wanted, still want, to find meaning, stitch together stories, turn history into an intelligible sea—and you scold me, with good reason, a reason that always falls short of this impossible science I am groping toward.

If voices could be displayed like the clothing in the fashion ads you loved so much, you would make up the entire catalog of masculine tones all on your own. You open every vowel to the utmost frivolity, then suddenly clamp them shut and whistle out s's like feral cobras. After that, you delve deep into your body to find the slow melody of emotions, which you wave in opaque scintillations over your paper eyes. Thus intermittently illuminated, your eyes shatter the full list of the characters you have lived. You drape your voice over the words in a thousand veils, because you know that discourse fails—a grain of vanity, two drops of falsehood, a modicum of modesty. "Screw it," you said. "Whatever," you said. "You've wrung so much out of life, kid, you've ended up getting wrung out yourself. Now there's not much left of you." The words made a brutal contrast with your Italian silk scarves. They deceive and soothe, words do. Like silk.

I go hunting for dazzling words, trip over them both inside and outside of life, interpret, get hurt, interpret again, sully myself, wipe the makeup from the face I don't have, the faces I used to draw on the face I lacked—but oh, never young people. I never knew what "young people" were, never knew what "my day" was.

I was always late to everything, remember? Probably so I'd reach death sooner. I died so many times before my death—I died every time love ended, and love was always ending inside me. It ended and expanded, consumed everything I knew. I imagined new sentences as dams against those empty spaces in which I floated. But the dams would collapse, I'd wash back up on the beach, dead, and be reborn to shiver with cold in the marine night. Then once more I'd construct my dam, clutch my past, present, and future dead to me, grow old and be reborn, wrinkled and starving. I talked. I talked ceaselessly about things I knew and things I didn't; I waited for people to tell me to shut up so I could just listen to the wind of the fundamental words dancing like a disheveled lunatic in my body's murky interior.

Where is he now, the imaginary friend from my solitary childhood? He used to dwell in my liver, my lungs, my belly and blood. Whenever I was feeling bad, I'd ask him to change out my fuses, scrub my pitted guts, and he'd obey. The chaos was temporary because that imaginary friend existed, giving my life a bit of reality. There's so little reality in a life—stray scraps of history, stones flying through the air, crashing into the stratosphere, short-circuiting our aims. I loved that short circuit, used to provoke it. So perfection could be achieved with a single burst of laughter—the mad joke of a mocking, permissive God. Young people don't think about anything but sex, say those who don't think about anything but sex; they don't know how to love anymore, say those who have forgotten the names of the people they used to love, those who have only loved names, those who have only.

You're not alone—can't you feel me, your real imaginary friend? Parcel out the pain I left you for the pain-starved, my dear, those who haven't yet been moved by suffering. In that task of bestowing beauty on posthumous days, you can secure my existence. There was an abandoned child crying behind a door downtown. A child who ended up starving to death, clawing at the door, without the neighbors—though they heard his incessant wails—doing anything. What if that child held the ultimate secret of quantum theory? There are so few people whose talent can save us—and we can't even find and save them. We take comfort in the immediate beauty of coincidences, while the catastrophic beauty of chance eludes us. At Machu Picchu, the Incas' descendants—children whose minds are misspent on the coins of poverty, their feet gnawed by cold, hugging llamas, garbed in brightly colored rags that tourists find picturesque—sell fissured smiles. If Einstein had been born in the magical mountains of Peru, would he have had the chance to grant us relativity? Deafness to the suffering of chance remains central to our oh-so-sophisticated animal science. Every tear you shed for me, shut away in your silent house, represents one less day of living for the next child who's going to die slowly, in picturesque Europe, without being able to know life's pleasures. The mother had been arrested while trying to buy heroin, and she telephoned a friend from prison, in a whisper, to ask him to go to the house to get the child. The friend wasn't home, so she left a message on a cell phone the friend no longer used because he didn't have the money to buy more minutes. One of the prison guards overheard the furtive message from that woman who would rather risk her son's life than lose possession of him.

It's in the Bible, you know, the issue of Solomonic judgment—everything's in there, however much you resist the idea. So the prison guard sent a hasty fax describing the emergency to Social Services, asking them to rush to the defendant's home to rescue the child. It so happened that the woman in charge of distributing faxes was on vacation. The department head, swamped with work and irritated by the excessive heat and her husband's laziness at home, bent to pick up the pile of faxes lying on the floor, scanned them rapidly, and tossed them in the trash without spotting the one that mentioned the emergency.

Thanks to this succession of meaningless happenstances, a nine-month-old baby ended up succumbing to hunger and thirst in a European apartment, until eventually the neighbors alerted authorities about the foul odor issuing from that floor.

But you stride toward death and give thanks to the natural order of things on every single one of your cloudless days, so you'll assign the blame to the organization of society. You'll sleep easy, nestled in the comfort of missing me. Dying slowly, particle by particle. I hear the sound of death on your skin, a book's pages curling in the humid chamber of time. Your organs cool—how long has it been since your heart burned?

9

Money. Abstract time, future time that doesn't exist. They hand it out to everyone, every night, on every TV channel. "Even the audiences," you used to say, scandalized. Poor kid, you were always getting scandalized. And every time, you'd rush to the computer and write a scathing opinion piece. A miniature tsunami that brought additional spice and readership to the newspapers and problems to your life. You were removed from committees. People stopped listening to you. They listened to you less and less, and you became more and more upset about it.

They almost gave you the boot once. A nine-month-old baby died of hunger and thirst when his mother went out to buy drugs and forgot about him. It took the baby fifteen days to die; he crawled off the bed to the front door and wailed there in a five-story building. The residents called the police only when they began to be bothered by the stink of what proved to be the baby's decomposing body.

In response, you drafted a bill saying that substance-dependent mothers who refused treatment would immediately and irrevocably lose all rights to their children, who would be put up for adoption. In addition, you decried the country's ineffective justice system and general civic disengagement, and you said the baby's neighbors should be charged with failing to come to the aid of a person in danger.

At six months out from the parliamentary elections, this attitude rankled your party's leadership and many of your neofeminist friends, who called you a dictator and publicly distanced themselves from what they called your "oppressor's mind-set." They tried to placate you by quoting the Constitution, which, your peers claimed, defended freedom, individual self-determination, and family above all else; individuals who were unable to exercise vigorous self-determination and were incapable of choosing their family adequately, as would seem to be the case with babies, had to resign themselves to the consequences of other people's freedom, up to and including their own deaths. They insisted that substance abusers are fragile souls, deserving of our support and solidarity, and that drugs are a crime created by society, for which All-of-Us-Are-Responsible-Amen. Besides, harsh deterrence methods don't work—especially because blah blah tolerance blah blah understanding of differences blah blah accidents are always going to happen.

You'd been about to win an award for your tireless work promoting women's rights, but the jury immediately withdrew the nomination. The lost award actually made you laugh. Over the phone, you let out one of those sudden guffaws of yours: "They hand out awards to anything that moves—cats, dogs, rats, chickens. It's actually an honor that they're not going to stick me in that sack. Besides, awards on women's issues are always given separately, on the immensely convenient International Women's Day, so as not to intrude on the importance of the male honorees on Portugal Day."

You used to call me out of the blue when you felt discouraged, overwhelmed by rage. "I can't sleep, it's so stupid. For two months now, I've been waking with a start in the middle of the night, hearing that baby sobbing even though I never met him. I go out to the stairs in my pajamas, swear to God, trying to figure out where the crying is coming from. One of these days they're going to grab me and ship me off to the loony bin—but this whole damn country is basically a psych ward for the criminally insane anyway. What more can you hope for?"

Victory, victory. What did I hope for? Just that rare joy—the one when you'd say I was right. When it came to children, you were worse than me. You took things hard. Foolishly, I told you so once: "Don't make yourself crazy obsessing over a kid who's already dead. At least the boy's up on the playground in heaven now—if not, you should sue that lazy-ass God of yours." It became clear that had been two hundred and twenty-seven kinds of stupid when you hung up on me. That child was still dying, little by little, inside you. You needed a lap, warm milk with honey. I left you high and dry that night—seeking the pure joy of having you inside us, the way you used to be. But going back wasn't possible. You never called me again, and I sat crying over you in the doorless dungeon of my own inadequacy.

Sweetheart—that award, they actually came and pinned it to your dead body. Hyenas. I bent over the coffin to kiss you and plucked the medal, with its funereal gleam, from your chest. "Awesome," you said. "Now go give that piece of crap to that little fucker—he'll love to know somebody remembers him." Incense-induced hallucination, I know, delirium in my anguish over you. Unreal reality, whatever, fuck off—I did hear you. Your voice. If it wasn't you, it was a fantastic imitation by one of those winged transvestites you used to believe in. I went on the internet looking for information on the baby's burial, found his name, and carried out your wish. He's got a medal now, your little Unknown Soldier. I'd like to see him in your arms, glowing in the light of that solar smile you'd beam across the clouds whenever he called you Mom. But you forgot to bequeath me that battered treasure known as faith. I don't see your blood in the sunset—only the blood of the infinite immanence where you no longer are. It is only on the path to your nonbeing that I resound. Without a heaven for your voice to reverberate in, how can I hear you?

10

And we disagreed on so much. You never seemed to do anything yourself, but you'd fiercely defend neoliberalism, claim you were being robbed when you heard about projects to support marginalized populations. You believed competence ought to be compensated, and it seemed natural to you that incompetence be punished with unemployment. At the same time, you railed against the young and wealthy who inherited positions and salaries through favors and recommendations. You got furious with me when I reminded you that you, too, had gotten a high-level job just because you came from money.

You argued for harsh sentencing for criminals, and you considered even people who committed manslaughter—who accidentally hit somebody while speeding, for example—to be criminals. Occasionally, having attempted to tally all the inequity in the world, you'd fly into a rage of corrective justice. "There's no peace without justice," you'd insist, and I'd respond, "If we're always imposing justice, looking for the righteous and the wronged, we're never going to find any peace." But I said those sorts of things mostly to get on your nerves, and entering politics actually made me even more justice oriented and unbending than you. Fruitlessly so—like you. Sometimes it was really hard to like you. You did it on purpose—you liked making it harder and harder to like you. It still is, or I wouldn't still be on your path.

10

On this game show, they're giving out cars in addition to money. The contestants have to guess how many times people curse, on average, per day. We're informed that it's sixteen times, and the person who gets closest to that number will be the winner. These things can go terribly wrong. A few days back, a scrawny girl won fifty million escudos for hitting upon, though merely by chance and with a sympathetic assist from the host, the name of Agustina Bessa-Luís as the author of *The Sybil*. She did three interviews to apologize to the writer and promised she'd go out immediately and buy that classic. She likes to read, she insists: at the moment, she's loving the best-seller *Five and a Half Flings*, by Rosarinho Clero de Sá.

I see you reading. You used to devour books, with your hands, your eyes, your entire body. You'd fall asleep on top of them, on the beach, in bed, on the sofa; you'd underline them, add phrases, exclamation points, question marks. You read everything, you said, but it wasn't true; I never saw you reading anything like *Six and a Half Flings* (or was it seven?). You were racing to catch up on all the Tolstoy, Cervantes, and Proust you hadn't been forced to read when you were young. Your reading was eclectic, that's for sure. You mixed Deleuze and Ruth Rendell. Castelo Branco and Duras and Chekhov's short stories and Montaigne's essays. Even—supreme heresy!—Shakespeare and Berthe Bernage. You were thrilled when, at a used bookstore, you came across all five volumes of *The Romance of Isabel*, which you'd loved as a teenager: "Just think, this is out of print now because it's politically incorrect. What's wrong with the story of young love between a war hero and a nurse who wants to save the world? People complain it presents a reductive view of women and blah blah blah. They're even harder on the Famous Five series. Those are being rewritten because everybody's decided it's bad that George is a tomboy. Do you think that's OK?"

My dear, dear Tink, how I miss having someone around who doesn't think everything's OK. You'd laugh at me whenever I grumbled, "This crap only happens to me." I got enormous pleasure from tallying affronts: power and water outages, potholes, traffic jams, incorrect change, bad service. I'd tell you all of it, in voluminous detail, and conclude: "This crap only happens to me." You'd laugh. "Poor baby. Let it go, it could be worse. You could have been shipped off to fight in Africa, you know." And I'd laugh, but I never told you the war stories you were hoping to hear. I'd tossed them into a coffin of silence and buried it far away from my life, long before I was reborn by your side.

There's a dog barking in the night. I'm that dog. Actually, I'm worse off than him because I know I'm going to die, and I know that my death is of absolutely no importance. Just like yours. Will I live long enough to forget you? Is your laughter on a carousel something a person can forget? Your voice on the telephone didn't last long—they deactivated your number within a week: "I can't answer the phone right now, but leave a message and I'll call as soon as I can. Thank you."

I should write the book we planned to write together. Or, rather, you planned—planning was always your department. After a well-irrigated lunch, I'd go off to digest my repast and you'd head up into the clouds and start planning. It pissed you off when I pointed out that no work of any merit had been written by two people. "So?

Electricity hadn't been invented yet before Edison. If you can't make the leap, just let go. Buck up, son."

You could spend hours at a time worked up about Portugal's problems. You never got used to the outsize malice in our diminutive country. And politics drove you batty. Without realizing it, you took the fado singer's traditional turn down the alleyway of victimization. You saw conspiracies and persecution everywhere. You wanted to be Spanish. You wanted to be English. You wanted to emigrate to Australia. And yet you'd roundly chide me, your old friend, when I complained that we'd had the misfortune of being born to the guys who stayed behind, not the ones who set out to discover the world. You moved straight from the World of Absolute Possibility to Obstacle Alley. But oh boy, when I said it.

11

What do you do in that prison? The sun is setting behind the buildings, cars honking in the city's clogged arteries, eager to return home. You're walking slowly—that's how you got here, on foot from your house, absorbed, oblivious to everything. They open the gates to you immediately, like they already know you. A few inmates wave to you from the yard. You go into a room with a blackboard on the far wall, the students sit down, and you pick up the chalk and write: "Introduction to Feudalism." You were a teacher too, much more than I was—you offered that gift voluntarily, and I never knew. You're still a teacher, even knowing that all knowledge arrives too late.

Too late. Those are the saddest words in any language. And yet you dance through your lesson, make the words into visible beings, entities in transformation; the students follow you, free once more, dancing with you to the marvelous music of history, the tremendous fiction of time that allows them to invent reality. Your students include murderers, thieves, drug addicts; one of them is practically a kid—you lightly stroke his hair.

In that moment, Marc Bloch's caress appears in yours, the hand with which he stroked the head of a boy sobbing, in the imminence of death, on June 16, 1944. That day when the Gestapo, which had arrested the historian and tortured him for more than three months, made him climb into a truck with other prisoners, *including the weeping sixteen-year-old. Marc lifted his hand, stroked the boy's hair, and consoled him: "Don't be afraid, it won't hurt at all." And as if the boy were contesting the veracity of that claim, Bloch insisted: "I'm a professor at the Sorbonne, I can't tell lies." And the youth dried his tears to die at Bloch's side. The tears that now, by Bloch's side, you turn into light. You, my disciple, who dwells in the night of my devastated thoughts.*

11

You never knew I taught classes too. In the frank eyes of these amateur criminals (because if they were professionals, they wouldn't be
behind bars), I read the hope-filled outline of your own eyes, my
oh-so-mistaken professor. Why would I admit to you my weakness,
probably naïve, clearly petulant, for feeling useful? These men cling
to knowledge as if it might be worth something. The feudal wars carry us far beyond these bars to the happiness of better and worse fates
than theirs. That's what history's for, in the end—a tonic of courage
that we dole out in doses proportional to our bodies. But where is
your body?

How I long for a heaven to place you in. They look good in heaven,
your too-long skirts and those wool sweaters you knitted. But night
hems in my attempts to think about you, swaths them in the world's
darkness. Maybe you're still right, even now that you aren't anything.
You used to tell me I thought too much—now I can't even think about
you. I always thought about you all these years. I thought about your
smile when happiness eluded me; I recalled with delight your inappro-
priate phrasings, which instead of gaffes became bright candle flames
during dark dinners. My friends thought you were an old man's fantasy, an inconvenient extravagance. Me defying the vast gulf of age that
united us.

Maybe there's no such thing as age, just dead people echoing down the channels of time, dead people who, like magnets, move close and then away from those who have not yet died. You carried so many dead in the shadow of your smile. A woven tapestry of the dead. Your passionate fury was like a vast funeral pyre, your surrender like that of bodies to the flames, a knowledge of ashes.

This night is studded with jewels, as you used to say. You always used over-the-top images—it is only in that excess that I now find a whiff of peace. Studded with jewels, the sky, above the delinquent sea of my youth. You weren't yet born when I used to dive into those cold waves at night to prove my manhood to the girls on summer vacation.

With you I could be everything I had it in me to be, before and after and on the margins of that task of being a man. Be or not be your friend, for example. Once we hit thirty, we stop paying any attention to the people who cross our paths. Like putting a sign up: Applications No Longer Accepted. In childhood, all it took was a kid liking the same kind of candy for us to ask, "Do you want to be my best friend?" Later, bestness ceases to exist—we enter the age of equivalencies. But for you there was always such a thing as better and worse. Well, fine, Tink, I do think too much, but you always judged too much. You believed in virtue, gave speeches about courage and generosity, dignity and humanity. My friends found you naïve, tiresome and naïve. You were tiresome, yes, but precisely because you didn't waste time being naïve. You carried your judgments, which could be cruel and unfair, to their natural conclusions in an effort to unravel the meaning of life more swiftly.

You weren't a good teacher—I can tell you that now. You failed to account for the slowness of other people's reasoning, the mental somnolence in which most of your students were accustomed to living. You made giant epistemological leaps, and anyone who didn't follow was left behind. You had a restless mental agility. I confess that often I myself didn't follow you, but I at least understood that there was no point in telling you that. Not even you could have explained those leaps; you soared over your subjects like an intrepid sparrow with aspirations to eaglehood. Yes, you were a sparrow convinced it was an eagle. Don't get huffy. The rest of us hop from twig to twig like sparrows; few dare attempt an eagle's plunging dive. I miss your daring. I miss you. I teach amateur liars—I can't tell you lies.

12

A tiny part of me is still trembling with passion behind a door where nobody lives anymore, where I never died. In these rooms where you never set foot lived a man, and his body was my dwelling place. But I didn't know. And here in this nolus, I can no longer do anything about that ignorance; I have no way of honoring the fleshly habitation contract we unwittingly established. Do you imagine a nonbody and beg for kisses, saliva, sweat, and skin? My only shelter is you, friend without a place of perdition. In you, the ultimate escape, beacon of safety, I flee from the passion that ripped me from life.

I don't seek out any of the other men I loved, maybe because none of them will have retained more than the fleeting taste of my body. They loved the newness of our pleasure, my smile, my passion, what I had to give.

Soberly, you loved what I didn't give: resentment, insecurity, motherliness. You liked seeing me fail, and it wasn't out of vanity or pity, as is often the case between friends. My mediocre side didn't rouse your noblest instincts. You simply loved the soil of me the way a child loves a pebble, a bite of gingerbread, a teddy bear with missing eyes. It's that love I'm missing now—yours, the everyday love of unhappy moments, gibes, absences. You used to take pictures of me when I was angry, disheveled, sleeping with my mouth open, licking the lid of a yogurt container. Or, all too often, with my eyes swollen from crying. And I looked good in those photos.

They're so ephemeral, those joyous complicities. Skin, ideas, atmospheres coming together, floating like clouds toward the paradise of forgetting. I used to believe that my life's meaning lay in those encounters, and I'm faced now with how much I miss you. You rob me of meaning, and I've become addicted to that theft—maybe that, too, is an addiction to meaning, the ultimate one. We were never accomplices—we knew each other too well. We were promiscuous. We challenged each other's mind-sets in order to touch the fog of humanity. You betrayed me—you betrayed me so many times and never even grazed the edge of betrayal. People used to say I forgave you everything. They were wrong. I never had anything to forgive you for, as I see now with impossible clarity. You enjoyed discord, which is a sort of instantaneous intimacy. As did I. We were unforgivable; we will remain unforgivable each to the other, shipwrecked hulls on the black conflagration of the sea.

12

Nobody remembers you the way I do. Your friends describe you as cold, stern, always swifter to criticism than to praise. And immensely concerned with image. They place in your dead mouth statements that seem impossible and then sigh pityingly: "Deep down, she was a fragile person. It's to be expected—she lost her parents so young." Summing you up in the space of three old postcards makes you easier to file away. Luísa, who was hired on your recommendation, now tells anyone who'll listen that she remembers when you arrived at the university. And nobody sets her straight. This feasting on your decomposed flesh is going to turn me misanthropic. I'd rather hang out at my club of old snobs—at least aesthetes respect statues' silence. Nobody talks about the way you smoked, cigarette held between the middle and ring fingers of your left hand. Nobody can describe the curve of your fingers, spirits in marionette motion. They taught you to talk without your hands; in TV debates, you'd shackle those spirits to a fountain pen. I used to stare at them tethered there, impatient to leap in concert with your words, to dance, transparent bodies inebriated with dreams. With those hands subdued, your speech became flatter, but I don't think I ever had the chance to tell you that.

13

I need to say good-bye to you, or accept death, which is the same thing. I was never able to say good-bye to anybody, not ever. My parents crashed on a curve in the road; I was fourteen and wanted to lose faith in God. I'd been taught that God gave in proportion to our effort—and God gave me his oscillating smile in exchange for my incomprehensible sorrow. The worst had happened; nobody else could take anything away from me. God had offered me the searing light of pain to intensify my life.

Pain needs a body. Boundaries of skin, nails, snot, sweat. The inability to leave, the irremediable courage to live time's passage. Patience, weight, brain on fire. I don't accept the death of immortality, and I don't hear my father's warm, singsong voice. It was so hard for me not to have a father when I started to become beautiful. A father with whom I could leap into the mystery of womanhood, a father I could butt heads with and then soften, bring boys home to and ask for help. At fourteen I was told I had no father or mother, told that nobody can claim to have the love she needs most. I called to them across the nights' saturated void and never heard their voices.

I hear them now, those inflexible voices, stripped of the relativizing veils of time. My mother tells my father, "I want a divorce from you. And from the kid. She's more yours than mine, anyway. The two of you have robbed me of the right to live my own life." God, why don't you rob me of my right to know this truth that never came to be?

I was treated well, extremely well, as people generally are when others feel sorry for them. Nobody ever scolded me; the world tried to be gentle with me. You were the first person to be rough on me. You told me everything you were thinking, especially when it was unpleasant. You even made up bad things to tell me—you enjoyed seeing me speechless, at a loss. But you never prodded the tender core of my weakness—you never told me, "You, too, lie and fail; you, too, betray and flee—you, too, are imperfect." You accused me only of being too naïve—and, occasionally, intolerant. You kept people who liked me away from me. Only now do I see that you deliberately shooed them away, impelled by the wretched, awful, emotional vulture of jealousy. Especially women. You used to say that women's affection for one another is artificial, and maybe you were almost always right. "Oh, sure, Ângela," you'd say mockingly, "her name might be angelic, but you'll see she's anything but."

And I started becoming suspicious of people in the shadow of your words; you cast darkness over others' every gesture toward me. "She gave you a blue dress even though that's your worst color. And no, it wasn't because she didn't realize—it was deliberate. She wanted people to look at you and think the blue of that dress would work better on her body, with her eyes." I came to see Ângela as you did, lashed out, and ended up without her. Later, after we'd fallen out, I found the two of you dancing in each other's arms on a night out at Lux.

I'd stopped talking to her because of you. One night you were arguing with her about a play she was in, a collage of texts by Camões and Pessoa that you deemed pompous, hollow, mediocre, and ridiculous. You always went all out when it came to insulting adjectives. Ângela's temper flared, I intervened, and she accused me of always defending you, no matter what.

The play really was mediocre. There wasn't much left of Camões, and Pessoa came off as an idiot, recited in those apathetic voices, clumsily sketched, a succession of white hands grasping teacups and wineglasses, rising and falling against the blackness of the stage like fat spiders. The director, in a dull, very young voice, argued that Pessoa hadn't had a body. Now Pessoa had a body, and it had come for all of us, unfolding multiplied, and it was that body that fed us; I found it in so many houses drawn by Pomar, by Almada, a bourgeois, status-building substitute for the Last Supper, taking the mental place of the Ches and Xananas for luckier generations. Pessoa may not have ever experienced sex, but why don't we consider him a superbody, a body in stereo, concentrated in its own dense eroticism? Why do we refuse to understand experiences that stray from the calcinated paths of action?

No, not that Pessoa, cut up and sewn into an inhuman spectacle, shackled to a naked Camões, with too much body for someone who had so little, who poured it into a fire that burns unseen. But I never could have told Ângela that. Out of friendship—or out of that cowardice we call friendship. When I failed to defend her, she turned on me with terrifyingly true aim: "You know the difference between good and bad! You just don't have any standards—that's why you hang around with an old coot like him!"

So I cut off my relationship with one of the women I liked most. Ângela became famous after that play, so I never got the chance to make up with her. It's always easier to make overtures to somebody everybody's forgotten, at least for me. I would see her glowing on magazine covers, and I'd feel the pang of that assertion: "You just don't have any standards." For you, insults were like burns: as time passes, a scar forms, and it's as if nothing happened. For me, though I was always so quick and impatient in everyday life, it was the opposite: the injury intensified with time, expanded, swallowed me up. You used to tell me, "Kid, you're so good that you provoke other people to be bad." I hadn't yet realized that badness is never other people's. You always adopted a jocular tone when you spoke—and the more honest you were being, the more you joked.

I gave myself to people back then; I gave the best I could, which is why I reacted so badly to signs of mistrust, malice, suspicion. I gave myself to other people because of you—yes, just to throw you off balance. When you admired a man, I had to seduce him. When you retreated into solitude, I had to set you up with somebody. I developed a group of friends to match your preferences, dropping anybody I thought you wouldn't approve of. I threw myself into everything you loved and pretended I was innocent, or at least perverse, so as not to lose you. Later, I threw myself into the resentment of not having you, into cursing you, not knowing how to be indifferent to you. And now I'm giving you my death too, so you'll stay by my side at last.

13

I'm tired of you. Tired of being tired of you. You wore me out, in life—you never stopped being, existed too much in everything, demanded of me at every moment. You were omnivorous, wanting to devour life in every way possible. I've gone out with so many women because of you—like that Ângela chick you tried to hook me up with, a C-rate actress who saw herself as a sort of intellectual Greta Garbo—oh, the long, boring hours I spent in theaters to avoid disappointing you! And yet you profoundly disappointed me when you got into politics. You didn't even ask my opinion. That was the only time you didn't ask my opinion—you knew I'd say being an assemblywoman was beneath you. When you decided the country needed you, you stopped needing me. At least that's how it felt. Your phone was always busy. After three days without talking to you, I started getting used to that new silence. I got used to it bitterly—and that bitterness became part of me. Your voice grew decentered, melodic. I couldn't stand the marketing-smooth tone with which you now defended the great causes of the universe. Where was my friend? Where was the intemperate, out-of-tune braying that used to serve as my rising sun?

Go ahead, find me a girlfriend. Come back to my life and set up your little matchmaking business—go on. Introduce me to yet another of those vulnerable Electras—make one of your shameless sales pitches, damn it. I'll be good; I'll take the girl to bed at your command, give her the best of myself to avoid disappointing you. The things I've done to boost your pride—poor goddess of our tiny urban Eden, poor, poor dear. I didn't want lovers or female friends or nights on the town. I just wanted to share with you the quiet domesticity of the two of us. I wanted to sit next to you, on a balcony overlooking the sea, and write a novel that you might admire. That was our shared project: writing parallel novels, our eyes mingling in the same sea. Because the story that brought us together, thoroughly wrung out, is good only for bad novels. Soap operas exploiting dead neurons.

You had talent, sure. The cruel light of talent shone in those half dozen stories you wrote—though you thought they were awful. "Terribly stilted," you'd say. "Every sentence in there cost me a life— and it wasn't even one of mine." You had so many lives. Sometimes it seemed I'd known you since high school. Often, I found you even further back, cradling my very first dreams, and I'd be tempted to call you Mother. The mother I wished I'd had—why is it we can't choose? My mother did me so much harm, and I could never choose her. If God existed, the bond between mothers and children would be something much more momentous than that cord of blood and grit. The maternal love I was given tasted like blood. It was a blind beast that trampled everything around me, all the loves I chose in life. As a kid, I was ashamed—all the boys knew how to run, swim, talk to girls. Except me. My siblings were born years after me, one right after the other, inseparable and pragmatic. We grew up without a father; my mother used to tell me he hated us, that he'd ditched us because he hated us. When I found the bundles of letters she'd saved, I wanted to kill her.

I tracked him down a few days before he left for good. He was headed to Sweden, where he'd gotten a job at an engineering firm. I wasn't able to challenge him—for him, I only conjured up memories of a docile child. My father had stopped imagining me a long time before. My siblings never wanted to meet him. He'd had another daughter and moved away with her and the woman he'd left my mother for. He had no desire to return. He was bored by Portugal; he'd participated in a few subversive plots against the dictatorship, but he'd ditched that too. "Dictators don't come out of nowhere," he told me. "They're earned. And we've definitely earned this one. People are still grateful to him for staying neutral during the war." He lived in a large, luminous house. I remember the windows were all open—I'd never seen so many windows, and so wide open. I cautioned him about catching cold from a draft of chilly air, and he chuckled: "Don't worry, Son. There's no air in this country, despite all the drafts." The furniture was made of blond wood. The walls were white, and there wasn't a knickknack in sight, just colorful canvases on the walls' broad expanses, many of them painted by him. And books, books scattered throughout the entire house, emitting a papery smell I never forgot.

It was an unusual house at a time when carpeting and flowery, baroque wallpaper had taken over the aesthetics of the bourgeoisie. My mother's house reflected an absolute terror of empty space: the antique sideboards gleamed with countless boxes made of gold lacquer, porcelain, crystal; the small tables in every corner were crowded with framed photos of all our relatives. We didn't have friends, just relatives, almost all of them dead or very far away. She'd carefully erased my father from all the photos, cutting them down to fit the tiny frames and encircling the remaining human beings in pink tissue paper, turning everybody into a sort of vaguely terrifying saint. I was particularly drawn to one of those images because of its bizarre composition: there I was, just two or three months old, smiling into the void, suspended in nothingness, wrapped in a blanket with a cutout of two absent hands. On my face, turned toward that absence, a besotted smile—a floating baby surrounded only by the faded pink of tissue paper.

My mother's room was her sanctuary. It was decorated with photos of me and my siblings, from every age. Often, they were just of me, abruptly alone. When she didn't like how she looked in a photo, she'd excise herself from it. She was meticulous about posterity and about appearances. I looked awful in many of the photos—wearing puffy shorts in one, a ruffled shirt in another—but she insisted on showing them off to anybody who came over. Few people ever did. I was terrified to introduce her to my friends, once I finally started having any. In that room, the images of my lonely youth were interspersed with pictures of Sãozinha, the folk saint of whom my mother was a devotee, and some portraits from her childhood as a Hungarian aristocrat.

She used to say that if she hadn't married my father, she'd have written a great work of literature about her beloved and long-suffering Hungary. It's true that when she married him, hastily, already pregnant with me, she didn't speak much Portuguese, and she did once win a literary prize in some kind of high school competition. But my father always encouraged her to keep writing. I remember stray exchanges— brusque, insistent. I would have been about four or five years old. "If you want to write, why don't you?" he'd ask. "What am I supposed to write in this deadly dull country?" she'd retort, irritated. I didn't understand those words—maybe that's why I remembered them. Maybe because the weight of resentment they held was too heavy for my age. Then my mother would slam a few doors, shut herself up in her room to listen to Hungarian music and cry. I felt really sorry for her. I felt so sorry for her that it took me years to realize that love wasn't an amplified sort of compassion.

Of course I loved her. Maybe my love for her was similar to hers for me: a bender of self-congratulation. Loving her despite all her faults, recognizing her pettiness and moral shortsightedness, made me a better person. Love as a means to self-aggrandizement. Even so, it was hard to listen to her interminable rants about her superiority and my genius. Embarrassing to hear her tell any woman holding a child by the hand that, when I was that age, I'd already known my times tables and been able to read. More wishful thinking.

That over-the-top mother of mine ended my first marriage. She used to write me endless letters in neat handwriting—she was immensely proud of her handwriting—complaining that my wife wasn't domestic enough and encouraging me to "be a man and put her in her place." My wife, who had the patience of a fisherman and was always sympathetically reminding me how lonely my mother was, read two of those awful letters and was never the same again. She was furious I'd never put a stop to those missives, that I'd let them go unanswered, as if I agreed. She accused me of refusing to take sides. Silence, intimacy—for me, that was taking sides. I was on hers. I never felt like that with anyone again. Despite what your friends say, sex loses us only when it is tainted by that addictive substance we call love. And in that sacred mystery—the only sacred mystery, at least before your death came along—there are no men, no women, no positions, no assembly instructions, no hotness ratings, no Kama Sutras, no yoga, none of that stuff. Just sweat, morbid substances, bodies in the surf, nothingness. Nothing that can be uttered, not even really remembered. I was effortlessly faithful to her, probably because she was so different from my mother.

Oddly, after reading those letters, she started resembling my mother more. She obsessed over domestic tasks. Her attention split; she wanted to be the ultimate housewife, not just a mathematical genius. It was the genius that fascinated me. If I'd stayed with her, I'd have moved to New York, where she was invited to join a research team—and I'd never have met you. And I'd be somebody else—so many shards of you are part of me.

Your joy was an incurable disease. I used to call you Tinker Bell because, like Peter Pan's fairy, you were sassy and sprinkled golden dust on everything you touched. But you were also temperamental and weepy, hypersensitive. And you had a vengeful streak, which eventually got on my nerves. But even what I resisted in you became flesh of my flesh. I adopted your loves and hatreds. I was your friend. I never got tired of you, only of your own exhaustion with yourself.

You changed. I don't know if it was politics, success, the mediocrity around you, or something else entirely. Your voice changed, your joy cooled, and I wanted you the way you used to be. You even changed your house. One of those celebrity decorators designed a new apartment for you. I never felt comfortable in that magazine home, all done up in white, blue, and yellow, right downtown. I still dream of your two-room apartment on the edge of the city. The musty odor in the stairwell. The back windows that looked out on a cement courtyard where the kids used to kick a ball around, ringed by other buildings with balconies full of canaries and clotheslines. All your old furniture expanded and shrank; the coffee table unfolded and rose to become a dining table as needed. Then you had to shove the sofas back to fit the folding chairs around the table. The sofas were upholstered in thick fabric with green-and-pink boughs. You'd bought them on sale at some department store. But you'd replaced the sofa-bed frame, made of sagging wire mesh, with wood so your friends could sleep comfortably.

There were always lots of people crashing in that tiny house. People would knock on the door and come up at all hours of the day and night. You would supply tea, cookies, comforting words. The walls were full of art, the frames almost touching—countless little drawings, watercolors, the occasional oil painting. Many of them were clumsy, amateurish. You said they'd been done by friends, lovingly dedicated, and that was enough for you. You even had a couple of sketches hastily drawn on restaurant napkins, and a collage I'd made as a joke one day with your old magazines, and which I begged you not to hang. Built-in bookshelves with a sliding door divided the living room from the kitchenette. On the right side of the tiny hall was the bathroom, then your room, with a bed perched high on drawers to make full use of the space.

I spent hours talking with you in the armchairs by the windows that looked out onto a field. You'd managed to squeeze in a little table with an electric heater. You used to claim you couldn't live without a space heater. A holdover from childhood. But when the decorator for the new phase of your life convinced you there was no room for the table, which was tacky anyway, you caved immediately. In that final political period of yours, the word *tacky*, which you'd previously enthusiastically embraced, made your hair stand on end.

14

Is it you I miss, or my own innocence when I met you? Suffering anticipates the pleasure of death, say the living, just to say something, when the inevitable draws near. And pain gradually separates people from one another. I didn't return the last kiss you gave me, the last kiss my father deposited on my forehead—

"You behave yourself, kid. I'll be back tomorrow. Don't get involved in politics."

That kiss you were unaware of sears the interior of your forehead; inside your head, I'm not dead, I wear micro miniskirts to piss you off, I seduce you and then tell you to get lost, I'm fourteen years old and I want you to die, then come back to life when my allowance runs out or I fall off my boyfriend's motorbike. I'm fifteen and nobody yells at me when I fall off that forbidden motorbike, when I lie and say I fell into the swimming pool; if I died, there wouldn't be any more need to honor my dead parents' memory—

"Be more careful next time, sweetie. Think of your poor parents."

I think about you, my poor friend, slowly devoured by ghosts, shedding the fear of death like snakeskin. When God gets distracted, pain falls on people's incandescent contours, transforming them into something else. A feeling of resentment. Leftover food after a party's ended. A poisoned pigeon in the grass. A flock of pigeons scavenging the city's remains. An armchair with a rats' nest inside it. The space they once had for surprise swells with heavy mud. All I know, all you know, are things like this: Once bitten, twice shy. Love hurts. Locking the barn door after the horse has been stolen. We are locked in the heat of stagnant waters, in the avoidance of life—and where is our light? Where is the pleasure of plunging into cold waters, of letting ourselves drift on the confidence of the sea? What distance is there between dislikes, which give the soul flavor, and the disappointments that gently devour it?

You're traveling. I'm accompanying you, in the place of death, along a truck-pocked road to that dusty village where they used to make drinking glasses. What are you looking for in that factory that no longer belongs to you?

"Do you need something, sir?"

You're looking for life before me. You're forgetting me. People used to say we talked the same, like an old married couple. I'd become crude, sailor-inflected. You were waxing lyrical and using aphorisms for everything, those sayings of mine you'd initially found so irritating. I could look at you and know the exact color and shape of your thoughts. Or at least I thought I could, which is the same thing.

I can't lift my hand to your face anymore—and I no longer have any idea what you're thinking. If only you'd look up at the sky, your eyes inflame this faraway nolus. Take me to your beach. Take to me the beach of your adolescence, while I was being born somewhere else. Take me to that beach where we were never together—we both loved the beach, remember? We'd set up a grill at the seaside, paging through newspapers, looking for tasty tidbits to make each other laugh. And how we laughed. You said that humor was humanity's defining quality—cats don't laugh, but even a member of the most remote indigenous tribe knows how to laugh at himself. You enjoyed laughing at me. It cracked you up to see me getting annoyed at gooseneck barnacles, the way they slipped between my fingers. In the shade of the boardwalk, the late afternoon floated, in a red slowness, around our warm skin. I never wanted you, but I liked imagining the pleasure of your body in other bodies, liked providing you with love affairs, introducing you to people who transformed you into a euphoric, obsessive child—someone more like me.

In you, passions grew like cacti—the contours of a face were enough to kindle your glow. And they transformed into cacti too, once the illusion had passed. "Women take longer to fall in love, but they're also more reluctant to end a relationship," you'd say, in a clinical tone you didn't usually apply to generalizations.

But maybe you were right. Women work at everything, even love. They demand endless rituals, conversations, a certain familiarity with mystery. They're much less tolerant of everyday unpredictabilities and face enormous disappointment with extreme calm. I used to get irritated by a myriad of tiny things that you'd gently take care of. But I was incapable of lying, cheating, deviating from my own truth, not even in order to brighten my life with a new face.

One day you almost vacated my heart entirely. You had a girlfriend I liked a lot who was far away, studying in Berlin. In the meantime, you were engaging in a quick, arid affair with a girl you'd met on a night out. You'd call your distant girlfriend at the appointed hours, repeating words of love and longing— and it was painful to witness how much the words of truth resembled those of dissembling. But one day you worked up the courage to tell her: "I've been going out a lot with a new friend, this girl I met at Frágil who's writing her dissertation on the image of Portugal in the nineteenth century. She's a real bore, poor thing. I even almost told her that, but I feel sorry for her, and I've been trying to help. Don't worry, there's nothing for you to worry about. She's got one of those awful mannequin bodies, you know. I'm not the least bit interested." We all lie, sometimes out of charity. But assaulting someone's trust so brutally—that can only be an act of malice. What you were violating was not just your girlfriend's trust but also the faith she'd placed in you. Ashes, a desert of parched sand—anybody who treats another person so badly doesn't deserve love at all.

Would you be capable of treating me that badly? Why do I still wonder that? Because I mistreated you too, egregiously. Your ideas, your past, the way my youth heightened your melancholy. I copied your essays, draped myself in their laurels, and forgot they were yours. And yet you loved me even more when I took you and consumed your soul, when I denied you in order to affirm myself.

14

The day disappears red on the horizon—another day of my life gone means I'm that much closer to you. "I can't answer the phone right now, but leave a message and I'll call as soon as I can. Thank you." I recorded your voice mail message before somebody shut it off for good. I was afraid of losing your voice. But it grows with your absence—entire sentences, stray bits of rage or happiness. And your smell. I gave the perfume you used to wear to a friend of mine. She put it on, and it wasn't the same. I left her and came home to weep for your irreplicable body. The gift of tears, which I lost in Africa and found again with you. You left it to me as an inheritance.

I'd like to write your life story, but what do I know about your life? While you were alive, I didn't need your story. But stories console us. I went back to Pinheirais looking for my own. The house that once belonged to my grandparents and my mother is now a supermarket. Instead of the rabbit hutches and the chicken coop, the blue and pink hydrangeas and the goldfish pond, they now park cars and shopping carts. The factory is still there, despite being on the verge of closing so many times. But it's run by Germans now, and I don't know anyone there. I prowl around it all afternoon and end up making myself look suspicious.

"Do you need something, sir?"

I tell him that, yes, I'd like to see inside the factory, I used to run it for five years. The guard is wary. He looks me up and down, gets my name, goes to ask. It takes him a while to come back—it must be hard to find somebody who remembers that time. Twenty years have gone by. What do twenty years mean? They usher me in. There are no longer men blowing glass—there are hardly any men at all, just machines. And they no longer make my mother's drinking glasses there, just endless lines of identical bottles. One of the old operators recognizes me, gives me a hug, thanks me. I look like an old man, I am an old man; you're right, I've lived to be much older than you at this point. Regardless, though, I'm touched by this gratitude, however much it's always made me squirm.

It cost me my second marriage, this factory did—at least, that's what I like to think. Though if it hadn't been the factory, it would have been something else. I was probably already tired of married life when I decided to become the communist Quixote, as my mother dubbed me. Yes, I was concerned about my nation's poor families. The idea of saving them was seductive, sure. But most of all I was driven by the need to keep my parents' legacy alive.

I offered to run the glass factory for a lower salary than I was earning at the bank as a lowly department head. Like you, I cared more about power than about money. I was already aware that my attitude would hurt my career at the bank—but in 1975, a career didn't mean anything. That was one of the good things about that tumultuous year—see how, deep down, though I didn't realize it at the time, I was already with you ideologically? My siblings wanted to take what our grandparents had built and sell it for a song; I managed to save it. We did sell it later, to the French, who later sold it to the Germans—but I managed to protect the factory's jobs and my family's name. And to sell the factory for a good price. I assumed that, in portioning out the money from the sale, my siblings would give me a larger percentage in recognition of my effort and sacrifice. But they didn't even mention it—and I didn't say anything. I never said anything to them again, actually—there were no more Christmases or birthdays together, and I never again heard the roughhousing and laughter of my nieces and nephews.

My mother was already dead when we sold the factory. Afterward, her house sat vacant for many years, slowly falling apart, without any talk about divvying it up. I gradually retrieved photos, books, letters— memories that nobody wanted and that had been disintegrating in the damp. Then one day a neighbor called to tell me a group of drug addicts had moved into the house. They'd chopped up the furniture for firewood, and the piano had disappeared.

For years I saw that house's suffering. Again and again I dreamed that the family had gathered in its ruins, lighting candles and building a fire in the fireplace, with the children leaping from beam to beam upstairs, the floor practically gone, the babies swaddled in blankets against the cold seeping through the drafty walls. We were pretending the house was alive and we were still the happy family of many Christmases ago. We would bring picnics, prepared foods in plastic containers; the house no longer had water or electricity, and plaster fell from the ceiling, snowdrifts of misery, of melancholy. My mother was alive and kept saying, "Isn't my house cozy?" She kept saying, "It's so good to have you here together."

In the final years of her life, my mother stopped lighting the fireplace. She said it was too much work to clean. She'd turn on a small space heater by her feet; the room was freezing. Dust had settled in a blanket of snow over the furniture. The house was starting to fall apart, which she knew but refused to admit. She spent entire days in front of the television, waiting for the phone to ring. And when one of us called, she'd lash out, her words caustic, about how lonely she was. Loneliness is contagious—it's a disease. And there is no cure. We started avoiding her—her and the house, so we didn't have to see them in that state. We stopped sleeping there. The bed linens were always damp with cold, the heaters didn't work, water seeped in through the cracks in the walls, and the wiring had become hazardous. We talked about fixing things up, but she refused. She didn't want to have the walls painted, said everything had to stay as it had always been—but nothing had stayed as it once was; none of us was the same anymore.

Only by living suspended above change could a person avoid pain; only by circumventing the monstrous perfection of time could one vanquish it. That's what I used to think—and I was deluding myself, because time is not thinkable. I focused on ceasing to be in order to be everything, on forgetting in order to control my existence. I am time; I am nothingness, the swift, still nothingness that shapes the body of time. Ceasing to be is still abiding by the implacable rules of being. I'm worn out from racing against pain, against memory, against childhood, against love and hate. I set a goal of tranquility that recedes as I run toward it. There is no peace in the moment, and I live from moment to moment. I've started to fear that peace feeds on the blood of the passion I have renounced.

You suffered so much, in the torturous marathon of passion. Show me how to suffer. Show me a pain that does not fade, that can gleam in the furrow of my tears once those tears have dried, that can leave a heaviness on the table where my head rested in despair. Show me the gentleness of that despair where past and future joys seethe, the splendor of mortal ecstasy. Show me your death, which in life I knew so little about.

15

There are some insignificant-seeming things we never forget. I was quite young, and that couple was, for me, the very picture of happiness. I was at that age when it's still possible to live happily ever after. They were radiant. Like they lived in a Gershwin song—rhythm, energy, color. I spent happy hours just watching them, wondering whether I'd ever enjoy that kind of harmony. I knew it wasn't likely—people know when they're misfits, even at twenty years old. They were the only married couple I knew—the only young married couple, I mean. They had a delightful son, interesting professions—she was a paleographer, he a psychiatrist. They didn't argue. They laughed a lot, about everything, about nothing. On the weekends, their house was always full of lively conversations. And one night, as we were going back down in the elevator, one of my colleagues said, "You know them pretty well, so spill: Is it true he likes boys and she likes girls and their marriage is a sham, a sort of secret deal they've made?"

The significant moments of my life didn't come back to me in the hour of my death. But now, floating in this nolus, my spirit, hungry for trivialities, takes pleasure in recalling these phrases, phrases I was never able to understand. Expressions of ingratitude, I think. How many similar things have I said, without realizing it? Because the opacity of evil is inside us. An unwitting wall in our hearts. We never see the harm we do, only the harm done to us. I know you always defended ingratitude as the invincible driving force of life on earth, but I never understood why. What the mechanism was. That understanding eludes me still, in the starry night from which I'm watching you, asking your forgiveness. I was so ungrateful toward you. I watch you now in the hope of discovering, at an unbridgeable distance from everything I was, the root of that wind that carried you so far from me. You were so ungrateful toward yourself. Toward your memory of me.

You were the first image in my brief death reel. I was rising in the hot-air balloon, when the light started melting and I heard your voice. You were saying, "Don't run away, Tink." We lived in Neverland, where people don't grow up so they never die. You laughed and assigned me the piercing dejection of a jealous fairy. "Don't run away, Tink." You said it really slowly, and then you were running across a field of blood, your slow feet fighting the wine-colored mud. And I wanted to tell you my name isn't Tink. I wanted to tell you my name, but I didn't have a voice anymore.

15

I tried many times to shut off one body in another, the banal trajectory of human nights. But I remember one particular occasion when I failed. I was with this beautiful woman, the opposite of the one I was trying to forget. She wasn't even really a person—she was a lounge chair. With features so perfect you forgot them even as you gazed at them. She looked like she was right out of a drawing handbook; the other one, the one I couldn't forget, had a gap between her front teeth, a slight strabismus, a hooked nose reminiscent of birds of prey.

They say beauty corrupts. For me, it is a blank canvas, innocent absence. I've met a lot of men like that, who are moved most by flaws. The women I've loved were an active violence against the principles of aesthetic harmony. As were the houses.

My mother's house. An overpowering odor of ripe apples, jam, red velvet, dented frames where sepia eyes closed to the mystery of life. They never smiled in those old-time portraits, with the snow of the Hungarian winters beyond the windowpanes, and the velvets and silver candlesticks. Moments of solemn posterity, staged to dazzle the unimaginable future.

Back then, the future was everything that exceeded the imagination. Now, the future doesn't exist; time was swapped out for space, where everything that was converges with everything that will be. That's called being contemporary. Living in the postmodern assumption of the infinite present, understanding everything without truly knowing anything. And you wanted to teach history, kid. One day, one of your students told you that all history is fiction so there was no point in outlining the phases of the Industrial Revolution. "All right. So it's also a fiction that I'm here at this moment looking at you, waiting for an answer. Get out." You had no patience for sophistry. You were exasperated by rhetoric. And you found half-truths unbearable. You were candor personified.

The plains of Alentejo looked like a child's drawing. A felted, undulating green sprinkled with red, white, and yellow dots. It was the first day of spring and we were on our way to Mértola with a five-year-old girl, the daughter of a friend of yours who was in mourning. The child asked us to stop and swim in a blue lake amid the green. We stopped, and you undressed the girl, put on the bathing suit you always carried in the car ("You never know when you're going to come across a good place to swim"), and strode into the freezing water with the girl clinging to you.

"Is my father up in the sky?" the girl asked as she dried off in the sun.

You reassured her that he was.

"All alone?"

You explained that, no, her father was with her grandfather and with your parents, who were dead too, playing cards. And watching over all of us down here. Then the girl wanted to play ball and then she fell down and got hurt, and you made up a story with cats, bats, and ghosts that made her laugh again. You were great at making up children's stories, with lots of adventures, excellent good guys, and terrible bad guys who ended up dying or coming over to the good side.

It used to devastate you that people were unable to inhabit a solid, unbreakable goodness. For example, you gave the little five-year-old girl's mother money, a lot of money, to build a darkroom so she could become a photographer. Then you hounded all the gallery owners in Lisbon to set up an exhibition for her. You suggested a topic: street children. You pulled every string at your disposal to make sure the exhibition was a major event: politicians, actors, TV anchors. And then she thanked her husband (who'd died of an overdose), her daughter, and the gallery owner for the inspiration. Not a word about you. Oh, my dear. You never learned to give for the mere joy of being able to give. For the divine power of standing outside to observe, with an intimate, omnipotent pleasure, the multimedia spectacle of human greatness and disaster.

I imagine you must have been hurt by our mutual friends' indifference to our breakup. They made no effort, however half-hearted, to get us back together. The friends you'd introduced me to said we weren't made for each other after all. That it had been clear from the start. One of them in particular started inundating me with little gifts, phone calls, messages. We called her Fish Stick after the foodstuff she used as a rhetorical flourish: "And as to that, fish sticks." One night you called me under the pretext of letting me know that a former colleague of yours at the university was getting divorced, having found her husband in bed with another man. Then you repeated that joke about how a modern woman prefers the Big Bad Wolf to Prince Charming because he sees her clearly, hears her even better, and finishes things off by eating her. Ten minutes earlier, I'd gotten an identical phone call from Fish Stick, who'd anticipated each and every one of your words without ever mentioning you. I didn't say anything, obviously. Why hurt you, when I was no longer able to soothe your pain? When even your retorts were gentler on me than you were?

Our friends were relieved when we split up. You were getting close to power; you'd become an employment agency with a bright neon sign, and they wanted all the jobs for themselves. And I was a bachelor, ideal for emergency exits. Or as bait for indifferent boy-friends. Apart, we were much more useful for the group of eccentric friends we'd assembled than we were together as lovers, glittering and dangerous. The people we'd created needed to kill us in order to survive. And we let ourselves be killed, because it's in love's nature to silently shatter, splinter into shards of glass that weigh on our hearts until death pieces it back together.

16

"Faith prevents us from living," you used to say. "It postpones all pleasure into the future—that's why the poor find it so useful." But how can we imagine pleasure without faith? When my parents died, I decided God was laughing at me and turned my back on him. The priest who buried them talked only about sin. Hell and contrition. The aunt and uncle who took me in told me my mother and father were in heaven watching over my future, and I became furious at those mute parents who'd left me in the solitary night, interrogating the stars. I never heard them, just like you don't hear what I'm saying to you now. But God's smile touched me, proving, in its swinging back and forth, that they were there, somewhere, in the blackness. And it seemed to me that the trick to existence was to look for voices in the night—a night whose tail sweeps along the bottom of the sea and through the interior of the earth, a night that the sun's white vapor opens only a little more. So I fell in love with books—with the night that invades us in them, when we open them, with the night that resists us in them, after we've read them, reread them, and shut them. With the night that continues, indefatigable, between the words, ownerless words, written from absence to absence.

16

Most of the time, people lie to protect us. When I asked about you, nobody had seen you. If I ran into you with one of our friends, it was just a coincidence, pure chance. We always think the world's much bigger than it really is. We always think too much—except you. That's what you used to say: "Stop thinking. You end up not understanding anything at all."

An innocent passion—inexhaustible. A sky that the blue didn't abandon, fastened there by the force of justice. You loved friendship with a bodyguard's devotion. Friendship solved the ephemeral arbitrariness of love. Silly girl. As if it were possible to explain the pleasure I felt in looking at your tousled hair dancing down your back.

You didn't want to change the world; you wanted a perfect world in which affections were as solid as houses. But houses die too. What would you do when you discovered that the world never actually changes, or at least never changes the way you want it to?

The blue sky changes to pink, orange; soon it will be black again. This is the excruciating hour, that time of day when the dead smell alive again before becoming a little more dead. I miss you. I see you walk past the café on the corner of my block, where I never came with you. I often see you at this time of evening. There are so many girls who look like you, and none of them is you. I see you in the mirror beside me, in my eyes, which look like yours, even in my habit of seeking out mirrors. "I spend my days imagining / Your shadow walking / From across the sea / On the other side of my sun / I thought I already knew everything / About this vast, tiny love / Contents and container / Far-flung as a lighthouse beacon." That faith you used to talk about is entangling me now, gnawing at me, in the banal despair of the songs where you now dwell.

17

I know you can't hear me. If you could, for starters, you'd choose another photo—I look so ridiculous in the one currently gracing your bedside table. I'm laughing too much—I'm all teeth, and I'm wearing an awful blouse with garish polka dots. I always had a complex about how skinny I was; I tried everything to put on some curves. But you liked to take pictures of me from the worst angles, in the worst situations—with my mouth full, coming out of the bathroom, with my hair standing on end, or recently awakened, bleary-eyed. When we'd go to the opera and I'd put on my best dress, you never took any pictures, not even when I asked. "Call a photographer from Hola magazine," you'd tell me. "Uptight princesses aren't in my wheelhouse."

You remember me, which is another type of listening—the only one, probably. Why is it that you remember me only now? Would I have had parents if they hadn't died? When I was a teenager, all of my friends complained about their parents, tried to get away from them. I wanted to hold on to everything. I lived every moment deeply anxious about the future—and look how my future turned out. I can't let go of that future I never had, made up of recollections of the imagined past. Now that you have a photo of me at your bedside, even if it's a bad one, I can leave you behind a little bit.

17

I thought I'd sleep better away from home. I sought the refuge of my childhood abode, which you never visited. But I can't get away from you. Everything is touched by you. You're in everything—night that's black or flooded with day, mountains, night of mine, night of ours, night of your absent arms. Think. Build a logical barricade of words against the terrible imagination of life. Organize memory on shelves, little toy cars boxed up for other little hands, other toys. Slough you off the way I slough off the heat in these ocean waves where quiet dreams of my adolescence sparkle. Recall myself before you—but you won't let me.

You rise up through my life with that abyssal laugh of yours. "My story's got to have a happy ending," you'd say, back when you still believed you could ward off death with words. "That's not in fashion, I know. It's easier to drift in the immediacy of sadness than to rend it until joy is disfigured. I'm sick of this world of aesthetes." You used to say that sort of stuff, prodding me just to see me buck. You won. I've become addicted to the joy of being with you, hunched over your words, burning for the first time with desire for your inexistent body. You won, Tink. Here you have me, agog and impatient, reconstructing the missing you in photographs, the conversations that perhaps we never had.

18

I'm looking for friendship that will make me happy. Saying it like that, it sounds laughable, and for good reason—friendship alone can't make a person happy. Nor can love. And if we succeeded in being completely happy, what would be left to desire? In any case, I was happy when there were four of us living together: me, Teresa, Silver Tongue (her boyfriend at the time), and Pascoal. It was like I was living in a children's story, the kind with three little pigs or seven dwarves, a small group that may squabble a lot but knows how to defend itself against a treacherous world. I believed in tribes back then. But the nest fell apart, slowly disappeared, leaving only a few tufts of cotton between my fingers—things that cannot be seen or snuffed out.

"I want to draw warmth. What does warmth look like?" Lia's daughter asked at two and a half. Corália had become "Lia" in an effort to leave behind not just her name but her origins. I was already protecting her back when we were in high school—first perched above her on the tender pedestal of pity, and later in genuine tribute to her faded plaid skirt. Students were no longer required to wear uniforms, the economy was booming, and American jeans were all the rage. But all Corália had was that pleated skirt, and she strode hero-ically across the schoolyard every day, trampling the girls' scorn and the boys' unwary blindness.

I need to find Lia, I need to say good-bye to Teresa, I need to hug the people who used to know how to be loved by me, all those who allowed themselves to be imagined by the precipice, fugitive creatures whose leaving made my shadow longer. Does some shadow of me fall across their lives?

I lean against the door of the house where I left my dead soul that day, thinking I was just leaving my flesh. The door of the house where a hundred times love held me, disguised as sex. There it is, lying on the floor where it started killing me, many years before my death.

18

You could have found yourself a widower who had his shit together. Somebody who'd be remembered afterward for the luminosity of his longing. When my friend Alexandre's wife died, he quietly asked me, his voice deflated, "Why doesn't death ask first, 'Can I take this person, or should I take somebody else?' I'd have told it to take me instead."

Alexandre's wife died of leukemia. He was a doctor and lied to her, confident that his faith in that lie would work the miracle of transforming it. Actually, there was no such thing as Alexandre's wife; it was Alexandre who was her husband, spouse of the painter who founded the neobaroque school and for whom love was not a singular noun but a plural one. If Alexandre had died first, his wife would have mourned him, painted him, and then forgotten him. But Alexandre lived off her blood, that unstable, fragile, over-the-top blood.

If death had asked me, I swear I would have begged it to take me instead of you. But I don't have the right to tell anybody that. Least of all you.

If God exists, he's one of those real snotty novelists—that I can tell you. The super-schematic kind who fires characters into whatever hole the market surveys have deemed most lucrative. That God of yours has gotten fat off the misery he's doled out to his unlucky characters—you should see them in Fátima, on their hands and knees, paying alms for the rare graces His Excellency grants them to keep their faith alight. You used to say that these crawling people, almost always women, live happily, in a restlessness of faith: "They are certain the Virgin Mary will intercede in the highest divine proceedings. Because she was a mother and saw her son crucified. Because they identify with her tears. Because she's beautiful and radiant as they have been and will be, throughout eternity."

When your parents died, people told you that faith is what saves us. What faith will save me from your death? You should see them, full of faith, on the via crucis to their offices, bent to their bosses' wills, ruminating on the coming Judgment Day, when the Lord will roll up his sleeves to avenge their interwoven humiliations. By declaring him dead at the top of their lungs, atheists made God a martyr—and up there, down here, everywhere in our lives, he is laughing at us, gnawing at your tender bones, gnawing at my body in which you breathe, drowning out the earthly music of your laughter with the thunderclaps of his boundless injustice.

If only I'd written down every day of our lives together, transcribed our conversations, grabbing hold of the time that was stolen from us. A narrative, an illusion of order that would stanch the inconsequential fluid of life. Just in case, see if you can make your Bewhiskered Imperialissimo understand that nobody liked you as much as I did. Maybe Mr. Big will settle you far away from the ungrateful schmucks you used to call lovers and will place me at your table instead, where I'll beat you at cards, as usual.

19

The friend with whom I was happy comes home, strips off her seduction uniform, folds it neatly, dons workout clothes, turns on the TV, and exercises on the stationary bicycle for half an hour. I asked her so many times to buy a real bike and go ride outside. And to try closing doors quietly instead of slamming them and accidentally waking me up. And to stop humming when I was watching the news. She'd laugh and keep doing all of those things. I think she thought they made her unique. Or maybe she enjoyed the rage those habits provoked in me. Whenever my irritation reached a boiling point, she'd start cracking up and I would soften. Nothing I did or said could drive her away—that was her power, a malign power that tested my limits.

We didn't last a month on our own. In a tribe, my desire to tear open that indestructible love slumbered in a timeless cocoon. I believed that I would find in friendship the mythic flavor of absolute correspondence, the synchronous happiness that love only approximates. But friendship also proved vulnerable to boredom and disappointment. Everything we touch falls apart. And then we become addicted to decay, the intoxicating perfume of dead things. You can sleep on someone's shoulder your whole life and live in other, separate bodies that never touch. Dreaming. That was always my greatest experience. I loved my dead parents much more intently than the real ones I'd had for fourteen years. That's what the dead are for: we can construct them to the measure of our despair.

I turned my back on the man who showed me the core of happiness because neither of us could embrace the vertical light of the proffered sky. We found ourselves in a culture that didn't believe in lasting relationships. We understood each other completely, and were amazed by that intimate understanding, which felt like a victimless crime. We were totally unfamiliar with the enigma of married life, its routines, the way passion is tempered by boredom. Being lovers, though, we couldn't live fraternally, nor, being soul siblings, could we live as lovers. Together, we were a single person amplified at least two hundred times. We didn't need anybody else. That's why it was so easy for us to take on new lovers so we could pretend that existence was continuing its usual course. I contemplate the improvised map of my body over time, and I can clearly make out its trajectory, the underwater organization of its movements, the black corridor of multiple deceptions.

I aspired so much to transcendence—and what for, when I can't even stroke the ears of the people I loved with the memory of my voice? Supreme Architect of the Universe, Babelic God of all bibles, grant me the blessing of a new life. Even if it's just on the back stairs of this painful, chaotic world I knew. Even if you increase the obstacles and disappointments I face. Even if you fool me again—the way you fooled yourself in sketching that life that could have been my child. You fooled yourself, didn't you?

19

Friendship, an endless history of forgiving. After a while, we lose patience with history, and we no longer care about forgiving or being forgiven. It's an exhausting internal aerobics, kid. You were so obsessive about everything. I wanted to filch that obsessiveness, to be twentysomething again, like you. But I was already old enough that I was becoming young again, like a child, trading one toy for another, drawn to the gleam in someone else's hand, existing on the surface of things, tactile. The sagacity of enjoyment, rather than the science of pleasure. Happiness wore you out, and suffering got you worked up; nothing was easy for you. "How have you lived so long and you're still so chipper?" you'd ask me. I'd just smile in response. Oh, if only you'd gotten to discover that living too long means ceasing to live. Children die in an instant. They don't hurt as much; they have no idea death exists. That's why I can't forgive your death. It pierces my bones. I am your death so that you can keep living. I needed a child who would make me mortal instead of just dead. A creature without past or future, today, here, in my arms that are swamped in your shadow. What of you will live on when I die?

I was bad at loving you, Tink. I wasn't everything you dreamed I might be. If only you'd taken my deficient love away with you to that land where you no longer are anything. But you insist on staying here with me, attacking me with the bared teeth of madness. Your silence crushes me. I no longer know how to seek out laughter, pursue momentary trickles of joy. I'm your victim, now to blame for everything I didn't do. If only you'd appear to me, just once. Turn into a ghost, sneak onto my balcony, show me your crumpled face. For many years, I longed to leave the country and become a foreigner. But now that my country is you, I have no way out. There are a hundred million stars in our galaxy alone. And your gaze exists in all of them, the cold glitter of the falsehood of me. Who am I, in this stupefying hell, black with your absence?

I pulled away from you because we were immortal; we would always return to each other. "I don't want children. It would be like being held hostage by someone else's life," you used to say. A child's death was the only thing you found unthinkable. You could have gotten past it if you'd found the right man. You were absolutely unbending on that score: a child needed a father and mother. And you detested women who got pregnant on purpose, with a criminal's calculated determination. Above all, you respected other people's freedom. But what is freedom? I don't believe in your God—I flee from gods who sketch all of life's sad thoughts on our newborn faces. I don't believe in anything that mars the smooth surface of life. You believed in everything, for better and for worse. My love for you is now reaching its apex. I have nothing left that I can grab on to. Not your body, not my mind, not life out there. The people who knew you are useless to us now. They remember you the way people recall a dead person. They make you up. I miss you. I can't manage to make you up.

Story lines, even the flimsiest, are rituals for escaping boredom. I used to tease you just to watch you squirm. I got bored listening to you. You got on my nerves tremendously, and I couldn't resist ribbing you. Mea culpa, mea maxima culpa, I can no longer hear your plaints. You never used existential hypochondria as a seduction technique—in fact, you detested it, got almost aggressive when anybody tried to sway you with imaginary complaints or maladies. "The only place I put up with that is in Woody Allen films. He uses hypochondria as background music, almost like he's apologizing for being so perfectly intelligent. Whereas most people use it instead of intelligence. Especially women, however hard it is for me to admit it." And you'd laugh. How I miss that laugh of yours. Almost obscene. It blotted out the daylight, the thrum of boredom, the shrieking of the kids downstairs. Later, you tamed it for politics—your smile had been dead for years when you died. There was something tragic in your laughter, a displeasure that the world was so unlike it. A whirling dance sweeping across pomp and poverty. A musty love that a person could dive into like an ocean of warm clouds. The eternal face of life was in that laugh that died.

20

"Keep the desires of my luckless body / The future of my warm blood / The soft light of my dreams / The space-time of undying passion." Pascoal was sitting on the seawall at Falésia, holding his notebook, looking for a new song, and I gave it to him. He scribbled it down as I dictated. Everything I didn't write, everything I could have written, the equation of the intransitive moment, was dictated to me by him. On the other side of the ocean, on a cold Canadian beach, my first boyfriend looks up at the stars, hearing me. Why can't you? I whisper Pascoal's song in his ear, and he murmurs my name. Without even knowing that I died. We no longer had any friends in common, and I never went to Canada. I ended things because I was too busy—we wrote each other often for a few years, then you showed up, and then politics. He leans his head on his shoulder as if he can hear my breathing. He's let his hair grow long—he looks blonder, less adult. I would go back to being something more than a sister to him if I could. I'm alive in every gesture he makes. But I can't be with him: I'm dead. Only in you, who returned after my death, am I unable to die.

20

Weddings, like funerals, are days for forgetting. We get drunk on champagne or tears, we drown ourselves in the ruin-filled riverbed where our blood usually flows, and suddenly it's nighttime and we don't really know what happened. Only afterward, from photographs, do we realize we were there—but nobody takes pictures of funerals. There are some photos of you from newspapers, a few seconds of video from a TV show, interspersed with archival images—politics has its perks. Then you appear, already transformed into a black box with Portugal's green-and-red flag draped over it—tacky to the end, even in the mystery of mortality. You sometimes lamented your lack of mystery, Tink—did I ever tell you that transparency was infinitely more seductive than all the layered veils of the divas you envied?

My dear indefatigable exterminator. You established a center for combating injustice, some bullshit department with a very proper-sounding name, the Equity Office, and what did it get you? It got you a rising flood of pain, dozens and dozens of women, beaten to a pulp, clinging to abused children, all coming to you for miracles—and you, inconsolable, inventing houses and schools and jobs that didn't exist, that never exist for unfortunate souls like them, you sleeping on the office floor, again and again, buoyed by the joy of other people's happiness, that fierce joy that was your greatest addiction. "Tonight, at least, they'll sleep easy. Tonight at least these women know somebody's protecting them," you'd tell me, in a sweet murmur, over the phone.

Eventually, you started receiving threats. Once, someone even tried to send a message by taking a shit in your bedroom. You laughed nervously: "Don't worry, these installations of outsider art don't scare me."

And so you'll become a gravestone etched with your name and two dates separated by a dash. At the stone's unveiling, somebody will call you a "notable figure." And nobody will mention the things that truly defined you: how you always went to bed really late because you loved the taste of tired words, the looseness of time uncorked by wine, and the darkness that allows laughter to flow. How you discovered, one sizzling summer back in high school, your calling as an out-of-work La Pasionaria, one of those people who, lacking a righteous war, devote themselves to nurturing their fellow citizens. How, in that role, you'd become addicted both to loving and to being loved, and how, like old Mother Teresa, whom you couldn't stand, you never doubted that Saint Peter would have a luxury suite reserved for you.

In the newspaper clippings, beside the black box in which they're carrying you, now turned to stone, I spot the shattered face of your friend Lia. In the caption, mechanical words of modesty or survival. In her eyes, the scorched gunpowder of shame. She voted against you, probably voted against her own past, when you pushed a bill legalizing abortion. And you never forgave her for that blatant betrayal. Yet you forgave, brick by brick, towering edifices of minor, repeated betrayals; are you not now capable of forgiving the wildly impassioned betrayal of that woman who put you at the center of her orbit? Didn't your Christ forgive the friend he loved most? Or are you unable to forgive her for the love you never felt for her—the love you wasted on incubated hearts like mine?

21

How rapturously we delude ourselves. I felt so selfless and pure when I joined the party the day after a brutal electoral defeat. "I'm in, whatever it takes," I said. I don't think anybody, least of all me, expected that ten years later, when we won the majority, I'd become an assembly member. You must have thought it was power or status that drew me. It never was. At least it wasn't fundamentally that. But it wasn't just loving one's neighbor either. Initially, it was more that variety of neighborly love that consists of failing to love oneself. Growing disillusionment with my little world pushed me toward virtue. After all, was God acting out of pure magnanimity when he created us?

I was fed up with the static poetry of coffeehouse revolution—I needed to act. I humbled myself in discipline and silence, acquired questionable business skills that made me proud. I learned, which is another form of teaching. A new indulgence of passion—the days passed without my noticing. Time, which had so often seemed lazy—though never circular, as you claimed—now came to me in pieces, a puzzle we could put back together with our little hands. An excess of historical study leads to passivity—at least, that's how it worked with you. The characters repeat, disappointments recur; human activity is just a pool full of showy fountains in which the water never changes. I analyzed laws, compared systems, planned endless projects, consoled by the well-being my efforts would bring to the world.

I withstood the soft fires of envy, machinations that interfered with my work and made the pages wither, but I kept going. When I stood up to speak at meetings, a buzz would run through the room; my comrades were affronted to hear a young woman demanding change with such conviction. Tensions would rise, and the murmurs along with them. On one occasion, I simply stopped talking midsentence, waiting for silence to silence them. Then I added, "As my comrades' attention span is very short today, I'll hand out copies of my speech instead so they can read it when they've settled down." I wrote a scathing opinion piece and submitted it to the press, accusing my party leaders of gender discrimination, which turned out spectacularly in my favor. It was an era that generously rewarded victims' heroic gestures.

Meanwhile, the Ministry of Health needed an image consultant, and Lia, on my recommendation, got the job. The government was trying to hire as many women as possible, and Lia had a background in advertising. Things were looking desperate for her: her daughter's father had disappeared months earlier, the agency where she worked had gone under, and she couldn't pay her rent and support her mother and daughter. I warned her about the political arena's bizarre quirks, but it soon became clear that Lia didn't need my advice. She was an Olympic medalist when it came to survival.

Within a month, she'd started dating the prime minister's chief of staff. And with such a degree of professionalism that she convinced herself it was love. Come summer, she bought a house in Cascais and appeared on the cover of a magazine, daughter on her lap, effusing about the glories of motherhood. I recalled her words at lunch when she'd told me she was pregnant: "I'm going to get an abortion, of course. I'm not about to screw up my life because of a few careless hours of fun. I'm just asking you to come to the clinic with me." I'd accompanied her once before, years earlier, when what Lia had thought would be her first date had turned into a forest full of famished wolves. A classmate had taken her on his motorcycle to 2001, the rock club, and at the end of the night had joined four other young men in raping her in an isolated area of Guincho. They left her stranded by the side of the road, warning her they'd kill her if she went to the police. Lia was fifteen at the time, and she didn't go to the police. The rapists were rich kids, the sons of prominent generals and lawyers. I paid for the abortion with what I'd saved of my allowance, and I didn't go camping that summer. I joined a women's movement and spent my vacation handing out pamphlets about family planning and rape culture.

Corália spent her vacation, as always, working as a waitress at a beachside café. She felt happy in the yellow-and-white uniform that made her exactly as pretty as any other girl her age. And she was saving money for her brilliant future.

21

Your fingers—could they be tangled in the wind, your fingers that no longer exist? When you did exist, the wind was just the wind. Everything had an exact form and a history of enduring beingness. I lost the toughness that enabled me to endure when I lost you—or, rather, when you disappeared and I lost myself in you. I scoffed at God despite all the fat, bearded things you swaddled yourself in, yet now I believe that the caress of your fingers is in the wind, the sparkle of your black eyes in the tears of a forlorn friend, in the stars, or in the sun's rays reflecting on the river. Friendship. I sketch your laughter onto that word and see you, all of you, in its place.

I spend my days rereading your favorite novels, the pages we underlined together. Graham Greene's *The End of the Affair*, which I found lying open, its cover torn, on an airplane seat many years ago on a trip to Goa. The girl sitting next to me discovered that someone she knew was on the plane and changed seats, leaving the book behind. It seemed that fate was smiling on me, because I'd forgotten to bring a book and I can't sleep on planes.

I'd never read Graham Greene, and after that, I read everything he wrote. But in no other book did I find the unspoiled amazement of that one, which spoke to me of a strange world—your world, where faith blossoms in a muted dance of subtle sorceries (you called them miracles). Your world, a world in which sin works as delicately as a makeup artist, transferring souls' dusky glow to the skin's warmth. A world in which evil, a gentle kind of vaccine, only makes the fever of human passions more beautiful—attenuating their traces, underscoring their risk and sacrifice. The girl left the plane without looking back, and I kept the book to reread it with you, years before we met.

22

Lia. In a black Chanel suit, at my funeral. President of the administrative council of the Portugalideal holding company. Leader of the National Women's Movement for Life. A practicing Catholic and converted democrat. Telling reporters that "though we did not always share the same ideas, we were bound by an unshakable loyalty." And that, without me, "democracy is the poorer."

I picture her on the night of the party vote on the abortion bill. I was giving a speech in a stifling room. I was gazing out at those rows of men drumming their fingers on their chairs, eager to leave, impatient to be wasting so much time on the pointless topic of women's abdomens. I was looking at the inextinguishable shine of Manuel's eyes when I heard a hiss, sharp as a needle: "I don't see why we're wasting time listening to this stupid extremist. We have to do what the people want, otherwise they'll crucify us." It was Lia's voice, followed by one of her strident laughs.

A few days later, I came out publicly in favor of the bill, against the referendum, and against voting in lockstep, and she called me irresponsible, a fossilized feminist and abortionist. That was yet another step in her meteoric rise in the party. And it was also the last interaction we ever had.

22

Your body, still so warm. Dust—according to your Bible it's now dust. That idea should be comforting, but it's not for me. I scratched your hand, hoping that a drop of you might still escape from your death to my life, bind us in a blood pact, with the brave levity of children. The heat still rising from your skin—could it be your desire for my blood? I finally understood our old buddy Camilo Castelo Branco; I wanted to profane you—if that verb can capture the urge to lacerate your skin so I might set it alight with the suffering of life, to bring you back to life with kisses or accompany you down the dank tunnel of death.

It was at the movies, remember? *Les Parapluies de Cherbourg,* an astoundingly kitschy film. You arrived late, appearing during the final swells of Michel Legrand's score, and I was indulging in the pleasure of tears. I used movies about quotidian tragedy as a semiannual catharsis. I'd disconnect my brain's fuses and weep in the darkness like a little girl, then emerge cleansed and lucid. You came in late and dropped, panting, into the seat next to me. Later, you told me it was in that moment that our eyes met. But I don't remember your eyes. I do remember the scent of your body, an arousing blend of roses, cinnamon, and sex. Maybe you were still covered in the smell of one of your lovers—you were a veritable archive of love affairs, and you were always ready to go dig for some forgotten information in an old file.

But I didn't know any of that then. And I'd never been so close to your body before. Your scent surprised me with its delicacy and its erotic charge. I propped my arm up beside yours and started to sweat. I felt an overpowering urge to fall on top of you. No, it wasn't about making love. There's no such thing as making love, damn it—love isn't something you make. Love crashes down on us fully formed; we don't control it—that's why our systems get so tired of replacing it with sex, a graphic, seemingly moldable thing. Nor was it about fucking, fornicating, copulating—those violent words we use in an attempt to destroy love. As if that were possible. As if love were not precisely that metaphysical fornication that has nothing to do with us—we merely suffer its splinters, which rob us of vigor and desire. I wanted to offer you my body so you could absorb it into yours. So you could make me disappear into your eyes. I, who'd been inculcated with the alimentary notion that boys eat girls, after an entire lifetime of controlling the cutlery, now wanted to be eaten by you. I wanted to put myself in your hands.

And I did—did you notice? I forgot who I was. Even now, I need you in order to exist. In order to sleep. One day, I admitted to you that I had insomnia. Did I ever tell you that Bach's *Goldberg Variations* were born out of a request from Count Kaiserling, who asked the composer for a cure for insomnia? That's why Bach wrote the variations in accordance with a formula that required "the relentless invariability of the core harmony." We used to talk late at night at your house, until you could barely keep your eyes open. I'd ask you to let me stay a little longer, and you'd take my hand—

"Come with me."

—and lead me to bed. You'd curl around me and start stroking my back very slowly. We slept like that many times—and we never, not for a second, thought of having what fools call sex. We talked a lot about it, sure—about the act that people call sex or love depending on convenience or circumstance. The act that people perform over and over again unto absolute solitude. But we couldn't do without each other. We couldn't enter into the infinite finite game of bodies. On countless nights, I poured my fleeting perfect loves, detail by detail, into your life. And you poured into mine your impossible, inextinguishable passions. And still I want you so much.

23

I see the wind stirring up the trees' spirits, pushing clouds along, cleansing the heavens—but I can't feel it. You hunch your shoulders against it in your jacket. If only I could control it, even just for a second, could give it the shape of my dead fingers and slowly stroke your tousled white hair. I follow you so that time will exist. Because you walk and look up at the sky and sometimes find that it's black, or glittering like a dark sea of jewels, or rainy, or sun parched, I know that the days are passing.

But I know less and less all the time. Suddenly, that passing grows elastic, and you, ponytail and all, become my first boyfriend, pointing out constellations in a distant firmament. I can't make out the contours of that boy during that period when I loved him, short-haired and perpetually dressed in black. But I am swept by a sudden vertigo because of those beloved bodies; you stand before me with the features, the movements, the gait of other men I loved in other ways. Oh, if I'd experienced this vertigo in life, I could have gone far.

Open up a book, please. Open Graham Greene's The End of the Affair and read me that scene where the two lovers separate after the first time they're reunited. Maurice lets go of Sarah's hand and walks away, without looking back, as if everything of any importance in the world exists in that other, nonexistent place toward which his steps are carrying him. But Sarah coughs, and, to fend off the hollow sound of that repeated cough, Maurice tries to imagine a melody that might drown it out, but he can't do it. *I have no ear for music,* he thinks, *I think now,* on the verge of the tears spinning on the CD player. "People can love without seeing each other, can't they?" Sarah used to ask, having left you in order to save you. Left Maurice, I mean. Same difference.

We can love in the dark, yes; we can love in the somnambulant light of absence: we invented God, after all. You used to say God was your favorite fictional character. But you refused to understand that fictional characters exist just as thoroughly as you do. Sometimes, many times, even more so. Read me the end of Tolstoy's *Resurrection,* tell me that Maslova went back to being Katusha, wearing a white dress with a blue sash, surrounded by candles, on the fervent night of that Easter mass when Nekhludoff loved her in her immovable eternity.

Read me the María Zambrano essays I taught you to love, tell me that "the heart is the drinking glass of love" and pour your blood into my dead, undying heart. You haven't learned everything yet, friend—you're taking too long. You still haven't learned to kill me. Everybody else buried me in the brightly lit cemetery of the TV news, effusively praising my dignity. May fame be gentle with them—I will be resting here in peace to forgive them that minute of glory. It looks so good on the screen, the grieving of the dead. But once that brief commercial known as life is over, everybody ends up here. The microphones swarming you: "I know it's a difficult time, but I'm told you were one of her best friends." You confirmed it: "That's why I don't talk about her. I just talk to her."

23

You died without a mother, without a father, without me. You died so alone. So full of love. I'd gotten out of the habit of you. At first, that break with habit was agonizing. I was dependent on your moods, your dreams, your inexhaustible activity. I was tired of depending on you so much, tired of having you do so much for me. I was tired of your red carnations, your swift, violent passions, the constancy of your so-certain love for me. I didn't know how to live like that. Nobody knows how to live like that, apparently: you died.

Did you die quickly, at least? I pray to gods I do not know that you did—quickly. An efficient angel to close your eyes like a puff of air, the brief opening and closing of a window.

You expected too much of me. You expected too much of life. You lived a high-speed Sebastianism I sometimes found exasperating. Nothing was going to change for the better—not civil institutions, or justice, or the Algarve landscape, or my face in the mirror. You loved me tremendously for what I wasn't; you pushed me to follow through on the crazy projects I dreamed up. And I enjoyed imagining things that would never exist.

My mother's house. I used to say I'd stopped visiting her much because I loved her and couldn't bear to see what she no longer was. She was dead five days without anyone noticing—it was Easter, the neighbors thought she was visiting us, and nobody called. Only when the bags from her morning bread deliveries piled up at the door did the neighbors reach out to us. I let the woman who brought me into the world die alone. She died suddenly. Deaths like that—swift, contemporary—are so easy. She was lying across a plate of potatoes. She didn't bother cooking anymore. The television stayed on, the sound turned way up, for five days in front of her dead body. Did I tell you I hadn't called her in more than a week? Neither had my Catholic siblings. One of them is a volunteer for a charity organization because he believes people's souls can be saved. How am I supposed to believe in an almighty creator when men (as in humanity, kid, please excuse the chauvinism) so closely resemble virus-infected computers?

"How can you talk about selling Mother's house?" the Good Samaritan asked me. He wanted to refurbish it, but I objected to that plan. Our mother had liked those stained pink walls, the creaking stairs, the persistent drip in the iron bathtub. Everything that had existed when we were children. Nobody visited her because her house was exactly what it had always been, but older, like her. She aged along with the house—she asserted her right to grow old, as you always put it during that phase when you were advocating a harmonious recalibration, in which everything in the world rested on the acceptance of each individual's rights. The right to die. The right to loneliness. The right to individualism, as long as it's orderly.

One day I asked you to host a French friend of mine who needed to get out of Paris to recover from a love affair gone wrong. Or at least to get a change of scenery. Love ends always and especially on tissue-paper stages that we cut to our own measure.

"I just can't right now," you said.

And I heard a piece of glass shatter. Somewhere in my body. With a nineteenth-century slowness.

"I just can't right now, you know. I have to prepare a motion for Parliament."

—Chantal's tears at having been traded in for a younger woman after twenty years—

"And anyway, I don't even know this friend of yours! We're not twenty years old anymore."

At twenty, our friends' friends were ours too. But now it was time to hear pieces of glass shattering, like tears, in my body's interstices.

"Why don't you cancel your little musical adventure and console your friend yourself? Come on."

I was silent; you must have heard the sound of the final piece of glass shattering through the telephone line, so you said it would be OK for a day or two. And since I'd already assured Chantal that you'd love to show her the castle, the light on the river, the Gulbenkian gardens, the enigmatic panels in the Museum of Ancient Art, and the new stars of fado, I seized on your reluctant charity and told Chantal she could come. But I think it was around then that I stopped wanting to call you. The joyous glow of our twenties had faded. I'd conjured another youth for you alone, one without betrayal or forgetting, without my so-certain death. I would survive in you, on the eternal battlefield of your memory. You would talk about me to successive generations of students, and I would live on in your stories when not even the dust of my bones remained.

You used to collect letters. Photographs. You underlined your books in green and red ink. You wrote in the margins. You weren't one to agree easily. You had an internal barometer that was pretty accurate in distinguishing between praise and flattery, provocation and offense. You seldom forgave. Though you were more forgiving with me than with others—at least that's what people said. There was a fundamental complicity between us: a loathing of ostentatious display. I might go overboard with my silk shirts and scarves, but you were just as snobby when it came to decrying contemptuous glamour. We used to delight in watching the parade of gluttons hopping from branch to branch, squawking an old-fashioned "Hell's bells" when they pricked themselves on a thorn, today forgetting yesterday's idols, perpetual fans of the next big thing, loving those who despised them and disdaining those who were fond of them. Or the wallowers, a gaggle of geniuses hamstrung by Portugal's small size. They always insisted that if this city were at least London or, ideally, New York, their talents would find real appreciation. We used to savor the green hue of the envious, the dark world of favors and ventures in which they moved, trading promotions and cursing other people's luck. How we laughed at those herds of highway robbers.

Now it's your absence that's laughing at me in the silence of my house. When you were alive, you could always come back. You hung in suspended existence over all the days we were apart. You were breathing somewhere in the same city. We might run into each other by chance one afternoon, in a garden, standing before a still life by your beloved Josefa de Óbidos. Sometimes I'd go out looking for you in the bars we used to frequent. And I'd return home certain that the sky would devise the exact time and light for that encounter.

I stopped answering the phone. With you, I'd lost the feminine vice of long conversations, reconstituting a body through its voice. I lost the habit of talking—I could write emails, but, with you, I didn't even do that. I miss you—have I told you that already? I read the Dostoyevsky novels you never had time to read, make you offerings of the torrents of guilt that flood my bloodstream with a hallucinatory anesthetic. It was fate, that grotesque swindler you called

God. You studied so much history, so many ways of scientifically shattering the blind cycle of eternal return, and there you are above the earth, absent from this spring that, without you, illuminates everything you loved. "But seeing everything means seeing nothing / Losing the thread at daybreak / With your soul all curled up / Like bait on a curved hook / In the clouds I see / A row of castles made for dreaming / Boxes of love where I can store / The things I no longer know about you / And my dark heart / Recites in future compassion / The pure poem / That time has placed in you."

24

You're the only one who still talks to me. Your fingernails scratching the skin of my hand—do you think I didn't feel that? That's crazy talk, of course. How can a dead body feel anything? But I'm so dead at this point that nobody will notice this madness. So dead that you no longer hear me, and I can tell you now that my bodiless body glows with desire for you. It happened in the candle-light. At that pragmatic hour when the crowd of sudden mourners of my absence headed to a restaurant near the church to mingle and you stayed with me, alone. You scratched my hand, seeking the blood I had traitorously allowed to dry. You scratched my hand and the guitar-playing fingers of my most intimate lover awoke in yours. In the skin where I no longer dwell, all the hours of mortal pleasure are kindled with ice. You stroked what was left of my now-vanished face, and the white blaze of the kisses that set it on fire so many nights vibrated among the candles.

Is the dead's desire for the living called necrophilia too? The candlelight, your face aflame above my remains. I had to die to desire you, I had to die to see the color of desire, that it's white, white and irreparable, like you, like the two of us. Like us. You were still caressing me when Isabel came in and whispered to Luísa, whom she never liked: "Look. He's just like her. Or she's just like him. Like an old married couple, a pair of obedient dogs." Bitches. They're completely untrustworthy, but they can see things they don't know. That's why I defended them so fiercely. That's why I got so sick of them.

Now I don't know how to get free of the fog your eyes have trapped me in. Cry for me and then forget me, darling, like everybody else. Cry for me and let me go. A lot of time has passed—I see it in your wrinkles, the way your body grows thinner as it dances on my memory. The way you look at that cheery girl in the photos, the girl I used to be. I died on you—that's why you look at me the way you did only that first time.

24

You used to think you were fooling me when you lied about your accomplishments and fame. You were hurt by the omniscient smile with which I greeted news of your disappointments. You told me you'd gotten tired of your last lover. You didn't want to see the bitter, contrary truth reproduced on my face: he was the one who'd gotten tired of you, more than once. The bastard. You were fooling yourself, kid.

You fooled yourself a lot when it came to people. You sketched everything in black and white. A moment of irritability, a regrettable choice of words—that person went straight into the trash can. Some of the women you brought me didn't deserve you. As soon as they stretched out on my sheets, they set to work trying to diminish you. They said you had delusions of grandeur. Considered yourself the ultimate arbiter of virtue. Couldn't keep a secret. Never shut up. As I felt them contort themselves, eyes intent and tongues like daggers, toward the beauty of my love for you, I lost all sexual interest in them.

Isabel even criticized the way you dressed, which she declared "drab and unimaginative." This, coming from a woman who couldn't dress herself without pictures from fashion magazines taped to the mirror. To whom you'd often lent money you never got back. For whom you worked your contacts, though you hated asking anybody for anything, to find her a job. She had the nerve to tell me the only reason she was staying on as a copyeditor was as a favor to you and your friends at the publishing house, knowing how hard it was to recruit qualified people for positions with so much responsibility. I had to listen to some amazing things, Tink, to escape from those harpies. What good would it have done to tell you all this? It would have fogged over those eyes of yours when I needed them as my beacons. And so I tried, without much success, to get you away from them. I think you hated me for that.

On the other hand, though she wounded you so deeply, Lia was a better friend than you knew. When thieves broke into your house and stole everything—stereo, TV, refrigerator, jewelry, money—she immediately called to give me a TV, a CD player, and a pearl necklace, with instructions to pass them on to you and pretend they came from me. I refused at first, feeling the request put me in an awkward position, but she kept pushing, claiming you'd never accept anything from her (which was true) and that it was the least she could do after everything you'd done for her: "Don't think of it as a gift from me. Think of it as simply a gesture of remembrance from my daughter for her godmother, to whom she owes her life in the first place." Expressed in those terms, in their powerful truth, the request felt impossible to refuse. Lia was merely getting rid of a tiny portion of the enormous sums of money she now possessed. So I told you that, by pure coincidence, some of my family's endlessly complicated inheritance imbroglios had been sorted out and that it was my great pleasure to present you with that small gift.

The anonymous checks you used to receive every month were from Lia too. Thanks to my skills as a postal archangel, you believed they came from an account belonging to your deceased parents that had suddenly come to light. I even took on the task of calling your aunt and uncle to set up that loving deception.

Yes, I know you'd be furious, even today, to find that out. On your heart's wobbly scales, only pride weighed more than generosity.

The pride of a little orphan girl raised by the kindness of an aunt and uncle who were always pointing out how kind they were.

Lia blamed herself, haunted by your retaliatory ghost. If money could soothe the pain of the suppurating wound of that guilt, who was I to deny her that relief? So few people are open to the martyrdom of guilt these days. Most people do without it, hoping to prolong youth, elegance, life. Afterward, they revile themselves for the spectacular life smiling back at them in the mirror—but it's too late to rewind and try again.

25

For many months we barely saw each other. We didn't look at each other. Until that moment when I sat down next to you at the movie theater. It was a French musical that hardly ever got screened anymore. It was called Les Parapluies de Cherbourg, and it started with a chromatic essay on the melancholy of dead loves. Your face turned toward mine in the intermittent light. Your clear eyes pulled me under like a wave. Your left arm slowly came to rest against mine, frame by frame.

Later on, we held hands in the movie theater many times, my head on your shoulder, sharing laughter and little secrets like high schoolers. But we never again experienced the pure pleasure of potentiality. As soon as I grasped your hand, I could tell we'd never make our way across the treacherous river of sex. Our temperatures were too compatible. With the great lover of my life, it was the opposite: I desired him from the moment his fingers touched mine.

But I have no doubt that we fell in love in that moment, in the movie theater. And we were in love again on that night when I lay dead in the candlelight, ready for the earthly feast, at the mercy of compassion and speeches about Life's Fundamental Values.

25

Guilt is what's left over after funerals—the true face of the dead, which expands and invades us. God is a conspiracy of the dead against the amnesia of the living. Your corpulent God looms over my mind, asking, "Why didn't you call her, you son of a bitch?" (God is an expert in belligerent vernacular, just as I suspected.) Shit. I used to ask you, "What have you been up to?" and you'd wave the newspaper in my face. The last time we spoke, in the middle of the night, you were gibbering about the death of a baby you didn't even know. And I, who knew you so well, abandoned you.

You won, Tink: the god of guilt has clutched my very core. But that wasn't the victory you were looking for, was it? The pleasure of guilt, that gastronomic pleasure of having pain we provoked linger in our own bodies. Or the swifter pleasure of sprinkling guilt on someone else's body. Guilt always needs a body. Now, for the first time, I need yours.

26

Values. As if they ever did anything for anybody. Some people have souls built for conformity, while others embrace change from birth. Those categories of spirit energy have a much greater influence on our trajectories than do the elaborate mental constructions we call values.

Take the aunt who raised me, for example. Her God was altruism, and she inculcated that supreme value in me. One summer day we were on the esplanade, thirsty, dying for a lemonade. There was just one waiter working the entire place, and he never seemed to make it to our table. After half an hour of waiting, I went up to the counter to order. The employee there apologized for the delay and told me our lemonades would be right out. My aunt scolded me: "We're not in a hurry—why did you make a fuss? I've never behaved that way in my life." By then, the lemonades had arrived, and I replied, with an irritated smile, "If you don't want yours, I'll drink it." And she snapped back, "I don't deserve this from you."

A couple of lemonades sparked an argument that was, at bottom, about how we saw the world. For my aunt, the rules were not to be questioned, and a person's attitude should be one of silent acquiescence. The ideal world was one in which everybody conformed to the established norms, making as little ruckus as possible. I think this accommodation of life was reinforced by having grown up in poverty, guided by a proud sense of honor whose first commandment was "Never complain in a commercial establishment, or they'll see you as inferior to other people. Plus, the employees are poorer than you, and you have to be magnanimous with the poor."

The other pillar of this worldview was spiritual accounting: everything given is noted down on the parchment of other people's souls so that, at the first opportunity, it can be duly repaid. As a result, the sums of the accumulated debt subtly gleam in any particular action, however trivial. "I don't deserve this from you" means "You owe me a great deal, so you have to give up this argument that I can't win." In balancing the ledgers of a relationship, there's no room for the unpredictability of temperament or the enigma of love.

Altruism—what does that word mean? It can refer equally to the systematic rectification of injustices or to the furious energy of revolution.

26

Another horror story—would God be in headphones at the beach while somewhere in a Chilean dungeon a little girl was being tortured in front of her mother? Answer me that, Tink. Can't you hear me? You feel far away. Remote and wrathful. It's like I can feel you, but I know I can't really. I'm just collapsing into my brain, which is drained from the ceaseless din of the television. I should have turned down the volume—where did that remote go? Silence might be even more painful. Music, sure—Wim Mertens's blue palette would be better. But making that improvement would require me to move, and just thinking about it wears me out. No, Tink, you can't make me move anymore. There's nothing I can do to change the spectacle of suffering, the hole that's left where your laughter used to be. Do you realize I'm starting to forget the sound of your laughter?

27

Truth. Another supreme value plying the seas of society like an empty luxury yacht. I lied to you so many times in faithfulness to the truth of my love for you. Or your love for me, which is basically the same thing.

It wasn't because I got tired of my last boyfriend that I left him. It was because I'd used up my youth, that capacity for, even when starting from ashes, nurturing a renewed and absolute belief in everything. For his part, he fell for that young assistant you were suspicious of. And she encouraged that fall. Darling. I had to be strong so you wouldn't worry about me. I had to be strong to be worthy of you—to annoy you, unsettle you, deserve your love for me. What are we supposed to call that, if not love?

It doesn't matter what we love. It's the substance of that love that matters. The successive layers of life incorporated into it. Words are only a beginning—not even the beginning. In love, beginnings, middles, and ends are just pieces of a story that continues beyond itself, before and after a life's brief blood flow. Everything is in service to that real obsession known as love. Dirt, light, roughness, smoothness, failure, persistence.

27

Belated angel, my jackpot, give me your wings and I'll give you happiness. Homeless, senseless angel, play hooky from heaven, keep me company. Fugitive, narrow-headed angel, perch on my lap and tell me "Good morning." Deceived angel, color of my life, come back to me or show me a way out. Angel of darkness, fearless bird, carry my sorrows away, tell me your secret.

28

The substance of love. In Lia's case: pearls, a TV, money. Substances she had to hustle for, and which she, ashamed, offered to me through you. It's only now that I see it. There's a photo of me in Lia's daughter's room, and I've only discovered that now. She will forget me more efficiently than you will. Or, rather, she'll evoke me with the sincere, garbled deference granted to founding heroes. She doesn't need me in order to breathe, like you do. But she needs to know I existed; she needs her daughter not to forget the godmother she no longer remembers. And that's love too.

When my house was broken into, she went to you, devious friend, to offer me consolation and comfort through you. A TV, some pearls, a little money. She did what she could—which wasn't much since I no longer let her anywhere near me. It's all written down in her diary, where she stores those memories that serve her no purpose in life.

Dearest God, how can a person wish to exist in you and yet be so blind in loving other people? You gave me the freedom to judge for myself, I know—and I turned that freedom into a prison, unable to escape the fish tank of my notion of love. Corrupt, career-driven Lia knows about love, about the transcendent forgiveness that sculpts its contours. Forced to choose between memory and affection, she opts for affection without a second thought. There was too much barren resentment in me, this parched desert, far from heaven and earth, from which I cry out an apology that she will no longer hear, especially since she never needed it. Lia forgave me a long time ago.

28

So many men killed you before you died—at least you didn't leave life without having experienced your share of euphoric suffering, that feeling we call happiness. I pointed out the faults in all of them to make sure you'd remain available to me. It wasn't jealousy; I found your romantic trials amusing, and I wasn't the least bit bothered by imagining you in their arms. But I had no interest in putting up with any of them for good, those mystery men you found so alluring even when you realized they were dopes. I didn't want to become your go-between. The most I was willing to accept, in terms of tripartite cohabitation, was a cat.

For a while there you had a remarkable cat: large, white, imperiously arrogant. When a human being approached—including you— the cat would hold its tail aloft and make off with a slow, determined gait. It didn't allow any kind of affection, hissing if anyone tried to pet it. Similarly, it refused to sleep on the floor—it slept beside you, on a pillow of its own at the head of your bed—but woe betide you if you attempted to pet it. I identified deeply with that cat's solitary personality; whenever you tried to put it in a basket to bring it to our weekend home, the cat fought so fiercely that you abandoned the effort.

I remember there was one time I wished the cat dead: you were making soup, and the aroma of chicken and mint was warming the house. We were chatting in the kitchen, by the stove, while the cat watched us with its polar-blue eyes, motionless on top of the refrigerator like a piece of china. One of your neighbors knocked on the door, and you opened it. The woman came in (she was retrieving a piece of clothing that had fallen down onto your clotheslines), and the cat panicked and dove straight into the pot of soup.

You laughed for a good hour once you'd managed to dump cat and soup into the sink and subdued and soothed the animal. Occasionally you'd say, "I'm surrounded by aesthetes everywhere I look. Even the cat, bless him," and then you'd start laughing again. That neighbor of yours was like the living incarnation of the evil queen in *Snow White*. Even her voice. "Can I grab a piece of clothing that fell onto your clotheslines?" she'd ask in the bleating voice with which the famous witch offered that poisoned apple. But your cat's aesthetic standards doomed me to a dinner of sausage and eggs instead of your soup, which was one of the few, if not the only, culinary strengths you had.

I don't know if it was because of the soup trauma that your standoffish cat escaped down the stairs one day when you went to put the trash out. It never came back, and you never wanted another one. You said you wouldn't be able to find another cat like him. Fish Stick tried to give you a pair of cute, gentle Siamese kittens anyway, and you immediately declared them "squishy and cloying" and gave them back. After that, you surrounded yourself with men. Chosen based on the same criteria of aloofness and self-involvement that you applied to cats—bless them.

29

I wanted you to forget about me. I know that wasn't right; I felt it acutely when the telephone stopped ringing, when the voice now sobbing inside the husk of what I used to be became choreographed. "What did you do yesterday?" I'd ask, and you'd spin three times and take four steps back, impeccably graceful. Damn you. You traded me for someone else, a new toy—that's how love goes. I was still in you, but you stopped needing me, which made me need you all the more.

I'd forgotten you so many times already—but they didn't count. I crawled into bed and cried for a week straight. Afterward, my boyfriend accused me of having "neglected" him. Nobody neglects anybody, nothing passes and nothing stays—that's just the illusion of time. It's still my love that lights up your face in the next moment of wonderment, like your first childhood crush, your marriages balled up in the pockets of old jackets that served as the candles for our platonic and carnal union. Flesh isn't sex, nor is sex as effective as it's claimed to be, you know. And you forgot me—I was already under your skin. You forgot me the way a baby forgets his mother. Or even the way a mother forgets her baby. The last time I spoke to you was during a bout of insomnia triggered by the heartbreaking story of a baby forgotten by his mother behind a door. I know that seems elementary; life is quite elementary. Death, believe me, is even more so—certainty, shadow, solitude.

Did my boyfriend fall for another woman because I neglected him, caught up in your abandonment of me? Causes and consequences, artificial comforts, sofas we use to furnish the windswept passageway of life—a false passageway, planks balanced above a motionless precipice. I've tumbled over the precipice now, my dear; nothing's going to happen to me. "The farthest you can fall is the ground," my gymnastics teacher used to say as I stood shaking with fright before the balance beam. And it's true, especially since there is no ground. Nothing's going to happen to me now, which is how I know that nothing ever happened to me—what events do we truly remember?

If you hadn't forgotten so much, you never would have remembered to like me. Most people choose memories to use as buoys: I was happy here, so here I'm going to stay, anchored in the middle of an immense, unknown sea. Or instead: I was happy here, so I refuse to leave. That's how you can tell them apart in day-to-day life, optimists and pessimists—professional rememberers.

How many friends did you have to forget, incorporate into your skin, to arrive at your love for me? How many words did you have to forget so you could say them for the first time? How many people are you able now, because of our love, to love better than the two of us once loved each other?

There's an exercise of feelings that can't be carried through to the end. A place where eternity sets in and the novelty of victories fades. A familiar place in a revival cinema that can exist only after death—as radiant remembrance. We had already been in that place. We were already only light, only stars, and, like stars, dead.

29

I can't really capture how much I miss you. Your friend Pascoal told me I should write down everything I remember about you. Even the insignificant things. The insignificant stuff is easy—that's the stuff you don't forget. The way you sought out every puddle and hopped in them like a child. Your love of rain, fireplaces, crashing waves, and the wind that made you whirl around on winter days. The noise of your lighter, which served as my alarm clock. Back when you smoked, the first thing you did when you woke up was light a cigarette. I used to hassle you about it because I didn't like smoke indoors and because, like I said, your lighter used to wake me up, there on the other side of the wall—the walls were so thin and the silence so deep in our peaceful home. Most of all, I hassled you because I was worried about your health. Pointlessly, I know—in the end, you died with your health intact.

The insignificant things are easy in their repetitive litany. Pascoal wrote that song for you, the one you liked so much about "The Shadow of the Clouds on the Sea." It's jam-packed with goddamn significant things—those huge goddamn significant things, which can be captured only in novels. And then only intermittently.

You've disappeared—I can't fictionalize you anymore. You're enveloping me like a cloud—I can't see outside of you or into you. And

I don't know what to do with what I see inside of me—dispirited substance, stuff of sadness and remorse.

Maybe I could escape this fog with an essay on the fragility of life and the blindness of ambition, but that wouldn't be us. Besides, I inherited from you the kind of pure enjoyment of life that runs out in just one page. I'd rather forget, forget you as much as necessary, to live as you lived, appreciating each moment—especially the painful ones, for the clarity they bring as a bonus—of this unreliable marvel we call existence.

I often counseled you on the virtues of silence. I wanted to shut you up to protect you. Few people are equipped for the truth—not even us. How many times did we keep our most cutting little truths under lock and key so as not to wound each other? I think you go *shhhhhh*—like that, with a lulling slowness—whenever the voice of my conscience (whatever that is) pipes up and criticizes me for all the things I failed to give you.

I believe without believing, like a condemned man. Ultimately, I have nothing to lose. Angels may not exist, but the wings I see, as you perch on the edge of my bed in the delirious heights of my insomnia, look better on you than any outfit you ever wore in life. I exert my imagination, stretch it out toward your fingers, but all I manage is the faintest caress of wings. It's just the bedsheets as I move them, I know, but won't you grant me the grace of transforming the hem of my sheet into your fingertips?

30

Listen. They're about to kill a little girl next door to you. Listen, please. LISTEN. You're engrossed in a TV special on Pinochet's crimes. You're horrified by the story of that four-year-old girl who was tortured for days in front of her mother in a Chilean prison. But it's just the surface of your soul that's horrified—you know there was nothing you could have done.

You take comfort in the conviction that you live on the side of good: you pay your taxes, help those in need, were willing to sacrifice your career for the sake of a bunch of glassmakers and your family's honor. You even give free classes to success's castoffs, those who rob and kill and take drugs and are in jail because they don't have enough money to buy freedom. You used to call me utopian because I wanted to refashion the entire world. But I didn't see you that way—I wanted you to remain small and contented so I could console myself with the idea that I was better than you.

You know it's not true that nothing changes. The world doesn't retreat every time it advances, following a fixed, chaotic order. One less death makes a difference. Turn down the TV—there's a two-year-old girl next door to you, screaming for help, though she doesn't know the words yet. And I can't do anything—I'm not anything. But you can, you son of a bitch. Get up out of that armchair, turn off the TV, please, and go to her. Do that for me.

The little girl's father hurls her against the wall, and she keeps saying, "I wa' go Grammy." The little girl's brother is hiding under the bed, quietly sobbing. He's five years old. The father pulls off his belt and lashes the girl, first on her diapered rump and then on her back, her belly, her plump little legs. He holds the girl with his other hand so she won't run away, and she says, "I wa' go Grammy." He beats her some more. He throws her against the wall and curses her. The little girl's crying is barely audible now, and you're completely oblivious. Everybody's oblivious, and she's going to die. But she's dying slowly. She says again that she wants to go to her grandmother; as long as she keeps repeating that sentence, the grandmother exists, and maybe the father who's drunkenly beating her will vanish into thin air, like in the movies she watches at her grandmother's house.

The little girl's mother isn't back from work yet—she's a night-shift janitor at a government ministry. The father will stop the beating only when the little girl goes quiet. The father's been beating the girl a long time—I don't know how many hours, but I know that time has started existing again.

People say we die when we want to. This theory always used to drive me crazy. I never wanted to die, my parents never wanted to die, nor does the young woman who right this moment has stopped her car on the 25 de Abril Bridge and is leaping off the railing onto the black cement of the river—she just wants to stop living, which isn't the same thing.

Get up, asshole. Turn down the volume on that sewer of images that's preventing you from seeing and hearing. Save the little girl who wants to go to her grandmother's, where Snow White and the Seven Dwarves live. Save her from the monster who gave her life and who tomorrow morning will go to the hospital to try to convince the doctors she fell during the night.

30

At least come and taste one of these tears I'm crying. Over you, over me—what difference does it make? I dried your tears so many times, damn it. Find a way to stroke my face with what's left of your hands— icy, blue, rotting; do you think any of that bothers me?

31

Children take a long time to die. Why do children take so long to die, God?

"It'll be over soon," repeats the brother, in the dark, kissing her, drinking her blood.

"It'll be over soon," repeats the brother, who's five years old and has an unrumpled faith in the healing power of words.

The little girl moans softly. She's already realized that the grandmother isn't coming, that the dwarves' house is too far away and they can't hear her, that her brother's words are going to remain alone with him. She's already realized everything, because she's dying.

"We're all dying," you used to say. But children die more slowly, forsaken by fairies and brave princes, in the pitch-blackness of a deranged forest.

There's a quiet police station on the corner, three houses down. Across from the window of the dark room where this girl is dying, there's a window all lit up. Inside, a little girl is playing with a cat as her grandmother works at her tatting and cries feebly while watching a soap opera. You chose to live in Bairro Alto because of this village feel: swallows in the eaves, geraniums in the windows, the sweet Portugal you lived in during your Salazar-era grade-school days. Later, you rejected that slow gentleness, calling it mediocrity. And later still, you grew nostalgic for the slatted blinds, the fado clubs, the inevitable old ladies sitting in windows—the good folk of Portugal.

Why is this death more agonizing than my own?

"It'll be over soon, it'll never be over, don't worry, every night is racked with violence, somewhere on earth, from the beginning of history to its end and its resumption."

31

Since you died, death has been hovering around me like an obsessive girlfriend. The kind that takes cruel pleasure in destroying our lives, sowing disasters in any space that doesn't belong to her, in the vague hope that one day we might understand that our peace depends on her whim. I couldn't save you.

Yesterday, my next-door neighbor killed his two-year-old daughter, and I didn't even notice what was happening. I couldn't even save a little girl screaming on the other side of my own wall—I had the TV turned up too loud. If it hadn't been the TV, it would have been a record, the radio, anything to fill the house with music or words. That's the first thing I do when I get home: turn on sound, doesn't matter what kind. I'm the ideal neighbor for a criminal. The perfect alibi. The affable executioner who until yesterday lived next door could spank and rape his daughter, the daughters of all the fathers in the neighborhood, with the protective complicity of my Bach or my nightly newscast.

Where did that little girl's future life go? What about the friends she never had, the loves she never knew, the particular projects of her singular brain—how will they grow up without her? Where do dreams that were never born reside? I'd stopped asking these questions after the war, questions that come to us, under the fire of all wars, when we see death dive-bombing bodies brimming with potential life.

I remember lying in the grass, gazing up at the majestic African sky and imagining that each star contained the energy of one life to use up, and that one day the stars would no longer fit into the night and would once more spill onto the earth in the form of a human race more perfect than the one we know.

I've never believed in any sort of God—particularly since, if I did believe, the two of us would have to settle accounts, which would mean immediately cutting off relations with him. But I believed intensely in the ontological talent of the human species. War taught me that too, taught me that above all: man (in the sense of humanity, of course, as I always have to specify with you) is the only animal that will die to save a stranger's life. I saw displays of true courage, generosity, and heroism, the kind we give kids to read about with their milk and cookies. I was pleased to confirm that such tales weren't pious fabrications. That's how I was able to share with you so many moments of amazement and rage, that vacillating, rapturous faith that constitutes happiness on this earth.

32

The purest nights. Those nights when I loved the greatest of my loves, the one who was never mine, the one to whom I never belonged because I withheld myself from him.

"Take and eat; this is my body, the one that belongs to the I that remains, dead and nameless, or maybe just decaying."

I decayed in that love, darling; it is in true love that we rot: ignorant, flesh-less, stripped of experiences and dreams, rising in the air like bone dust. I didn't come back from that love, nor will I. I'm not looking for it now, my dear, because I know I'm contained in the hugs he gives his one late-born daughter; I know I lurk in the sex—so sexual, so sad—he has with the woman he chose for life. I know I'm in him like a luminous trace of death, and I don't wish to see him in life because his life never had anything to do with me. "That man's so dead he's killing you," you told me one day—but I'm the one who was dead, dying at a rapid clip, greedy firewood, impatient to heat the world faster than any other fire.

He slowed my combustion. He could spend a whole night kissing just my pinkie finger. And that after an entire evening of leisurely conversation, savoring old stories. He always said that people who talk about themselves too much wear themselves out faster. And so I started to wear him out. I wore him out to the point that, after me, he started looking for a life. A history that would allow him to end ours. When we made love, it wasn't time that stopped. We were the ones who were already dead, infinitely dead, floating inside each other in a blue without sky or gravity.

He'd retreat and then seek me out. I'd retreat and then call him. He never called me—he'd pretend to run into me. He picked apart my words, one by one. After a while, I talked only so that he could destroy me, letter by letter, and his animal laughter drove me far away from men. He laughed like a cat—Alice's cat, a whereless smile. The smile of someone who was never a child and so never leaves the place of childhood, which is the place of death, the place without a yesterday or a tomorrow.

He is in me and in the death of the little girl whose father killed her; he is in me and in the death that his daughter is painting on white construction paper—here is a house, a dog, a garden bench. He is in me and in the son who killed me. Here we were happy; here we learned that we could never be anything again. I loved you with the scraps of that happiness, dear friend, which I accumulated like old clothing, notes passed in class, yellowing ticket stubs.

32

Blue, icy, washed by a distant sun—I'm going back to your cemetery today. True cold: the caress of the dead we loved dearly, and almost always inadequately. It's impossible to love completely except in memory. The stories we shared with the people we loved are reborn in slow motion on the vapor of our breath. Icy stars melting at the touch of your fingers. You never felt cold and saw shivering as a sign of spiritual weakness. You hated coats and scarves. You never got sick. You liked diving into gelid waves, your voice booming with the power of the sea itself. Near your still-fresh grave, the epitaph of a man who should have been me: "Here lies someone who never wanted to die, who had the misfortune to be born a man, not a god."

33

Only by listing dead things can one avoid dying. Our dead friendship, look: an unblemished photograph. What's left of it is everything we never said. Everything that kept us apart, the period in which we no longer existed. That's what never dies—what never existed.

That little girl's childhood didn't exist. The blood dried; the body cooled, livid as marble, trapped in dreams that have already been dreamed. This little girl who yesterday, right next to you, was sobbing for her grandmother—only now do you discover her, in the TV news shows' gallery of horrors, on display for the posthumous pleasure of noble sentiment. I was told that these tragic cases were the exception, the unpreventable exception. I slowly got used to incorporating them into the order of things, that immutable order.

Too many children are murdered every day for us to be able to do anything about it. Everything that's written, thought, done—all of it runs on a parallel track, the relentless track of frame construction. On television, a phalanx of veteran sociologists, psychologists, and therapists frame the little girl's death all night. They explain it, their voices hushing. They think the grandmothers of little girls who haven't yet ended up dead will stay quieter if offered these explanations. Sprawled at the base of the cliff of explanations, the little girl is still dead, violently dead, from a death that—like true love—will never stop happening, never stop haunting the fears of the living, their loneliness, their infinite capacity for killing slowly.

The difference between life and death may be a TV with its sound turned up loud enough to drown out another death. If I hadn't died, you wouldn't have turned the volume up so high. And you would have heard the child's screams, and she wouldn't have died.

33

I'm giving you my Venetian pitcher—I bought it to remind me of you, but it never did. Back then, I thought your house was primitive, with its hodgepodge of expand-and-shrink furniture. I liked giving you things. Or, rather, I liked giving you objects, indulging in the illusion of beautifying the lives of the people close to me and deepening my presence in their homes.

I gave you so many things: Visconti's *The Leopard*, which I'm not sure you ever watched; Richard Strauss's *Four Last Songs*, which elicited shrieks of delight when you opened it, saying you loved waltzes and weren't familiar with those. I found the record two months later, its plastic wrapper still intact, a virgin stone in the endless Tower of Pisa of your record collection. You blushed and stammered a shameless kicker: "Oh! That's weird! It's sealed. Even though I've listened to it a million times!" I gave you a beautiful edition of Mariana Alcoforado's *Letters*, which you lent to a friend and never got back. And a letter from Virginia Woolf, which cost me an arm and a leg at an auction in London, and which I ended up finding in one of your drawers, mixed in with bank statements, floppy disks, keys, candy, and internal party memos.

I wanted to take you to Venice, but you never seemed to have time. You never redeemed the travel IOU I gave you for your birthday. Days and months passed, and my desire to make that trip with

you waned. I ended up going with Fish Stick and Little Pig One instead, the kind of erratic outcome that tended to happen with you.
In a way, though, I was still honoring you. And I bought you this
pitcher that I'm leaving on your grave—now, at least, you can't let it
walk off in some chick's claws.

So you're dead. All that energy wasted, kid. You wore yourself
out with political infighting—what for? I warned you: "The word
state is masculine for a reason, and it's the real loser-y type of dude
too—why would you want to get involved in that?" You replied that
freedom is feminine. Just like revolution. And democracy. And
equality. I could add: and envy, and intrigue, and betrayal. Words,
balloons that add color to the void. But I didn't even feel like teas-
ing you anymore. Pity. You were pretty when you got annoyed. Or
embarrassed.

You were happier at the university than you ever were in the
legislature. Silly girl, you thought you could create a more just world
through sheer force of will. You weren't motivated by power itself,
though some status symbols did reel you in. Small but fundamental
things like that battalion of secretaries who used to call and leave
me messages. When I objected, you lost your temper—you had a
lot to do, you needed to use your time efficiently, that was the kind
of trivial thing secretaries were for. Politics altered your voice: it got
rough and rapid-fire, your laughter curt and forced. Another reason
I stopped wanting to call.

Your body is feeding the earth now—it will exist in the green of
the leaves. And in the scent of the wind, the physical substance of
days and nights. I look at your grave and feel your black eyes being
devoured by maggots, your bright smile rotting moment by moment,
your hands decomposing, disappearing forever from this world that
still belongs so much to you. Sunlight no longer caresses your skin,
and few people remain to truly mourn you—a handful of friends.

Nobody who saw you crawl, babble your first words. Your childhood sailed off many years ago, in the accident that killed your parents.

Was I your father? Could I be your son? What do you want from me? You come to salvage the pathetic disarray of my love for you. I wasn't able to dissolve into you—but I also never dissolved you. Did you at least know that, kid?

34

Writers cut out articles about these cases and think, I'm going to write about this. Words like puzzle pieces—in the end, the world again looks like it did in early childhood, the dead girls lined up on the shelf alongside ghosts and bedtime stories. Writers barricade themselves in storytelling to escape suffering. The suffering comes first, and then they write as a sort of revenge. Eventually they become skilled enough to write instead of suffering—the characters suffer for them and, with luck, for their profit.

I once came across a writer crying. At least it looked like she was crying, there in the bathroom during a break from an important political meeting. In my naïveté, I thought she was crying because of the way the men always put us down. They'd look right through us. They'd play deaf. They referred to us as "the girls"—the segregation of our school days seemingly irreversible. "On behalf of myself and Madam President of the Chamber, I'd like to state our absolute support for the victims of this flood," the councilor of public facilities announced in front of the ministers and the television cameras. "The councilor of tourism and I have decided to speed up the development of tourism infrastructure." The two women blushed and stayed quiet, fearing ridicule—and their subordinates beamed, applauded by the Greats and called to by dueling microphones.

When I told you about it, you shrugged: "Well, they shouldn't keep quiet. Speak up, damn it, regardless of how it looks." And maybe we really should have talked until we went hoarse. But it wasn't just that. Since I'd been a teacher, I was appointed to head up an educational field center and, soon after, was named *president of the Juvenile Protection Commission. Every day I saw new cases of kids who'd been beaten and whipped. The children of successful parents who forced them to kneel on nails when their grades dropped. Rich children who went hungry and were lashed with belt buckles to teach them discipline and competitiveness. And I'd intervene as best I could, delicately, pondering how little Marx had understood of human nature. Until one day I stopped being able to just ponder.*

"Please help us. He comes home drunk, rapes all of us, and then beats us. At this point we wouldn't even care if he raped us if he didn't beat us so badly afterward."

She was a twenty-four-year-old woman with broken ribs and a shattered face, the mother of three girls and two boys.

I called all the powerful people I knew—Minister, it's extremely urgent; Mr. Secretary of State, do me this favor; Director General, please give me a minute of your time—and managed to rustle up the funding to start a shelter I called the Equity Office. It accepted women and men alike to avoid the temptations of paternalism. Besides, other kinds of shipwrecked souls were drifting in among the successive waves of women with pummeled faces—Eastern European immigrants, exiled Gypsies, the handicapped, the elderly, people without anything or anyone but pain.

At first, everybody thought it was a fantastic idea with great media appeal. They gave me a cheerful office full of communication devices, arranged an opening ceremony with pomp and televisions, urged me to act. I acted with such energy that they decided to create an Equity Ministry—but uh-oh—the tide ebbed, the threats of economic crisis and unemployment reappeared on the horizon, and the press started talking about the bureaucratization of the state, how politicians were inventing pointless ministries like that equity one, when obviously equity should be a basic principle for every ministry.

Six months after its birth, the Equity Ministry was dead and buried. And I was brusquely advised to "stop stirring shit up," to quit making life more complicated for the party and the administration. "Why are you trying to shove all that crap in people's faces? Violence has always existed and always will—let democracy and the regular authorities take care of it." Since I wasn't willing to drop my battered women, my old men, my paraplegics, my abused children, they dropped me from all the committees, removed my staff, my funding, my access to power. They pulled my police protection, thinking that would intimidate me. But the guy who'd been harassing me, flooding my cell phone and home with threatening messages ("I'm going to fill your nose with acid, you whore, that'll teach you to take women away from their husbands"), he disappeared too, perhaps discouraged by my increasing insignificance. Or maybe he was actually part of the law enforcement structures that were supposedly protecting me—after all, weren't some of my women and children's domestic tyrants police officers?

Whenever I complained, they told me to shut up. Or they'd toss me a little crumb of power, a scrap of funding, a few personnel. "Just keep quiet," you'd tell me when you started realizing you actually liked me. "Because of who you are, you have to keep quiet, or you'll never get anywhere." "Because of who I am, I can't keep quiet," I fired back. "I'm the only safe place I know."

You insisted, though. I shouldn't declare myself a feminist in public. Or at least I should wear a tight, low-cut dress while saying it. I should smile instead of criticizing. Or at least smile while criticizing. Poor friend. It was for my own good, I know. Everything we're supposed to give up being is for our own good. Couldn't you see that the only good I wanted was simply the freedom to be who I was?

The writer was crying, holding a mascara brush in her hand, and the mascara was turning her tears black. The writer was a member of the European Parliament, a respected jurist, a critically acclaimed author. In political meetings, no one listened when she spoke, just like with the other women. But she was used to it—or maybe she wasn't. Those men never made me cry. It was a point of pride for me. I stopped crying when I was eleven. My father used to come home in a rage and slap me. He stopped the day I decided to ignore the slap. I just kept doing what I was doing, as if the violence had never happened. Politics was very similar to my father's homecomings.

"Let it go," I told the writer. "Place an op-ed in a newspaper. They'll have to read it if it's in the paper."

She laughed.

"I'm crying because Sousa Neto dumped me. I'm crying over him, practicing how he's going to cry in my novel when he tries to come back to me and it's too late."

See why I ditched our childish plan to write novels? There are so many of them these days, so many just a hyperrealistic falsification of reality. Oh, my dear—at least you were never a Sousa to me. You big lunk. Old thing. My dear. Baby. Fathead. Baby's the one thing you couldn't stand me to call you—which is why I did it so often. Your name was already worn out when I met you. Too many women, too many secret codes cracked too many times. And I never called you by your last name the way my girlfriends did. That writer even called her lover by his last name, Sousa. And he called her by hers, Fraga, like a man. That's what they called each other, and she felt respected somehow.

34

I bury myself in the books you left me, in the many books I loved because of you. Dazzling books where others wrote your dreams and nightmares, your anxieties. I underline the few sentences that haven't been underlined already. But none of them comfort me, now mere literature in the deadly tidying of history. I owe so much to you: Several lives, the multiple lives that appear in books, my life as a web, a map of shortcuts between nerve endings that came to make sense through books. My youth, restored at rock concerts or Brazilian nights at the Coliseu theater. My dancing skills, which warmed my body. Above all, the illusion of desire in the eyes of the women you reeled in for me—a redemptive illusion for men of my generation, raised with a religious obligation to love. You, the militant Catholic, taught me that it's not a sin to seek nothing more than the purity of mutual desire— you taught me to see purity in everything around me.

You appear to me now in dreams, sobbing, asking my forgiveness for the dissertation you "copied" from me. I want to respond, but in the dream, my voice won't work. And there are lots of people; I lose you. We're at a massive party on a verdant mountain with scattered ruins where all of our friends and acquaintances have shown up. All I want is to tell you this: if even once I was able to improve the orchestral arrangement for your melody, then I'm the one who should be grateful.

35

What is respect? The antechamber of fear. The back room of love. The tissue that remains after the body is gone—death, stitched tight to the terror of life. Don't respect me—don't forget me. "I respect the choice you've made," you told me one day, sitting at a table in one of those fancy restaurants where we'd meet from time to time once I went into politics. As if you were saying: "Now that you're exchanging our adolescent boardwalks for this well-heeled life, I'm not interested in the things you do." You stopped criticizing, no longer took leering delight in needling me, which a person does only with those he loves, the pleasure of guilt-free wickedness, the absolute erotic pleasure of conquest without victory.

Thanks to politics, I got used to living life as a sort of respectable game of chess: I'd let two of your pieces advance and then counterattack. I'd spend your birthday in silence, waiting for a complaint I knew wouldn't come, and then surprise you a month later with a bouquet of flowers. The first time we spent my birthday together, you gave me a videotape of Visconti's The Leopard and a postcard of Venice on which you'd written, "Good for two plane tickets and two hotel rooms in Venice." You wanted to be able to teach me something too, I think. Maybe you'd noticed that I—like the rest of the female sex, of course—had succumbed to the power of your beauty, and you wanted to show me that you were more than a handsome face. But you never took things any further—that's how manipulators behave and dominate, through faintly sketched gestures, like the dancing of fireworks under the impassive blackness of the heavens.

I'd call you out as a way of drawing a distinction between us—mirror, mirror on the wall, who's the purest of them all?—but I was no less skilled than you in the art of manipulation. "Disciples aren't enough for you anymore, you need voters," you told me with disillusioned rage in your eyes. My cheeks burned as if slapped; I felt insulted, as people do when their truth has suddenly been demolished. As we were walking into a café one day, you tossed a five-thousand-escudo bill into the hat of a beggar who was always sitting on the sidewalk by the front door. The man thanked you, overwhelmed: "May God carry you to paradise, sir." You explained to me that you went to that café every week, but gave the man alms only occasionally: "I prefer to give him a large amount every once in a while, to make sure he doesn't forget me."

Was I anything more than what that poor man was for you, a useful paving stone on your road to eternity? Were you anything more than that for me—isn't it teaching that brings us closest to eternity? Yours was a futile effort in the end—when I died, it was too early for the alms you occasionally tossed me to have secured your future.

My funeral was packed with pathetic souls—some five hundred people dressed to the nines so they'd be seen paying me their respects. Real pros in perfectly calibrated condolence and auspicious beginnings, who weren't stingy in their praise and harbored no embarrassment on their faces. I longed to kick them out, the way my fiery Jesus did the money changers in the temple. But you, my poor friend, with disheveled hair, a black scarf askew, and mismatched socks, were the flamboyant, flesh-bound image of sorrow. And I never said thank you.

I should have done so at the end of my dissertation defense. Even if it was only after the committee's decision, only after I'd been given summa cum laude honors. It was your research on prehistoric fertility cults and the increasing centrality of sex goddesses and priestesses in them that served as the foundation for my study of prostitutes' pioneering role in the struggle for women's liberation. It was your passion for ancient Greece that led me to discover the real Greek tragedy of the daily life of Athens's women, and the avant-garde influence on classical philosophy of the hetaerae, or "men's companions," highly educated and independent prostitutes, considered to be emanations of the goddess Aphrodite.

You were the one who made me see the extent to which postfeminist movements had revitalized the stereotype of the repentant prostitute, promoting it via a marketing campaign identical to that of the Catholic Church. You were the one who made me see that, contrary to popular belief, the unrefined Middle Ages, by keeping men busy with wars and crusades, actually increased women's freedom of movement, while the much-lauded Renaissance kept them trapped at home.

I copied your work and called it inspiration. When everybody stopped clapping, you hugged me with the strength of an unshaken affection, an indestructible pride—and I nestled there, lost in happiness, relief, and shame in your arms, with the words thank you shuddering in my throat. And I didn't say them.

35

I never threw you that surprise party you fantasized about, kid. An optimist, or an unrepentant cheat, I was going to do it for your fortieth birthday. With forty friends, obviously. But once you got involved in politics, things were more complicated: I had to comb through the mass of people around you to figure out how many were actually friends. You'd become a woman of influence, which really means a girl to be sucked dry.

People even started asking you to write forewords for them. And you'd do it—puffed up at first with academic-literary flattery, and later exhausted, with the disquieting sense that you were being hustled. Some even rounded out their requests with a Góngoresque tangle of words to make sure you realized what an honor it was for you. And you, out of breath, kept saying yes to everything.

You sunk your teeth into those who loved you and put them to work making phone calls. If only you'd stopped thinking about yourself for a second and wondered how many of those people would have kept hovering around you, hoping for another lunch date, if you hadn't had any favors to do for them. You had things backward: you said your mission on earth was to improve people's living conditions, but most of your work involved improving the living conditions of those who'd had it made since birth. And that was your surprise party.

Children's laughter lacerates me the way your parboiled cat would have liked to. I avoid parks so I won't hear their chorusing shrieks—you rise out of that laughter, wearing a pinafore, with a scrape on your nose, and you laugh, your front teeth missing. Your death has brought me my imaginary childhood. I'm playing marbles with you in the courtyard of an unfamiliar house, and your mother is scolding you—"It wasn't enough to be a tomboy, now you're bringing boys home"—and I give you a kiss on the forehead, and your forehead is a sea of rough wrinkles, you're missing your front teeth because you're very old, and you start laughing again: "Yeah, I am a tomboy."

I know so little about you. Our friendship was made of the present, of comments on the today shifting around us. Neither of us had family to visit—your parents, who'd been dead for so many years, were just a pretext for fabulations; the aunt and uncle who'd raised you, mere ceremonial figures for you to honor at ceremonial events. The only member of your family I met was the jealous God who took you away from me. Don't ask me to forgive him, because I can't. The only way I'll do that is if the Big Dude someday carries me to your feet—pull some strings, would you?

36

Why do I choose you, in this endless thrumming? Why do I long for you in my sleep, when you illuminate primarily what I never was? You died on me before I died—and I can't manage to die without you. I never could. Every day of my life I was with you—as if all my prior friendships had been merely the path leading me to you, as if all my later friendships were merely your absence. More delicate, more rhythmic, more clear-cut—less you.

I organized my love affairs. That's the primary rule in life—you've got to know how to file them, understand them, recount them, forget them. But nobody tells us how to survive the fading of a feeling that refuses to fade. Friendship, like one's homeland, is lost only through betrayal. On a battlefield, during active operations. There's no explanation for the disappearance of desire, the last and only lesson taught by the most extraordinary love. But when love is shielded from the deterioration of the body, nothing but scent and contour choreographed around the rainbows of that animated hope that we call soul—why does it vanish? How is it that, from one day to the next, your voice stopped seeking me out and I allowed my life to stop seeing itself reflected in yours?

We used to spend hours on the phone. Detailing all the day's events. Speculating on the hidden causes of our lovers' every gesture and word. Planning ambitious projects that would make us immortal geniuses. Listing the bad characteristics of good people. Methodically skewering bad people. Tallying up the ways we were the best and the worst in the world. Listening to the most beautiful tracks on the records each of us had acquired most recently. That's why I was never able to see the difference between men's conversation and women's. You were as much a woman as I was, and I was as much a man as you—and the two of us had sex, of course, everything between us was sex, sublime sex, without the creaking of springs, the fatiguing of bodies, without the melancholy ritual of frenzy and rest that reduces passion to ashes.

Did you get tired of my body, even in the abstract? On what day did you abandon me? With what word did my voice take its leave? What darkness opened within your eyes to shatter my image? In my nightmares, a vulture used to circle around you and eat your brain. You'd laugh if I told you about it, and say, as you often did, "Shrinks are never going to get rich off of you. No offense, but your subconscious is like a porno. Everything's all out in the open, all moans and whips." I was never able to live without you—I encountered you in all my dreams, on the brink of an explanation that never came but that I knew existed. One day, at our next lunch of convenience, you'd say, "It pissed me off when you did this or said that." And I'd tell you it wasn't intentional, and we'd go back to being a tightly tied knot.

It wasn't intentional. If I stopped moving you, amusing you, inspiring you, darling, it wasn't intentional. If I lost the ability to hurt you and make you bleed, it wasn't intentional. It wasn't my intention to copy you to avoid losing you, to keep you from realizing I might not be capable on my own. It wasn't my intention not to be capable—lazy, timorous, hiding in the cave of impossible perfection. It wasn't my intention to die, instead of swallowing some pills and picking up the phone to tell you I was killing myself.

I could never be that kind of woman. I was always tough as nails. I remember Teresa telling me her first boyfriend had despairingly complained that she wasn't willing to commit suicide over him. He ended up marrying a girl who attempted suicide three times in his honor. Of course, not even you deserved such treatment from me—I kept talking to you in my silent living room, with every tear, until death decided to come looking for me. But don't worry: it was just a coincidence, and it took nearly two years of conversations like that, in a silence inebriated with old laughter, for that coincidence to happen. And it wasn't intentional. If I'd imagined that even in death I'd still be crying over you, I would have gone looking for you in life to kill you.

I wrote you letters. I never sent you the most honest ones; they weren't brilliant enough, and I wanted you to think I was brilliant. The others, which were literarily unimpeachable, got no reply. Salvation was my department—you weren't that arrogant. You loved for pleasure, because only pleasure provides the art-madness that is love. My love for you was tinged with narcissism and will to power. You gave only what I asked of you; it never occurred to you to run, fire extinguisher in hand, to save me from fires that I hadn't even spotted.

I wanted to save the world. And yes, I also wanted to be seen saving the world. I had very precise ideas of how to go about it. I knew exactly how to encourage civil servants to give their best, how to do away with the privileges of the wealthy and distribute the world's excess among the poor, how to bolster young people and lower crime rates. It was all a matter of simple ideas, a massive investment in human ingenuity, which nobody seemed to believe in anymore.

I also knew exactly how to put an end to my friends' sadness or loneliness. My house was always bustling. It hurt when someone would tell me, after I'd spent the whole night healing hearts,

"You're not capable of living alone"

in an insidiously paternalistic voice.

I'd hoist up a smile with an imaginary crane, thinking about my books, the exams I had to grade, the condition I was going to be in for my meeting the next morning. That battered heart was there to do me a favor. To gulp down my whiskey, my free time, the most generous part of my heart, just because I wasn't capable of living alone.

I'm certainly not capable of dying alone. Nobody is. But we die better when we don't hear death tapping on our door, when it bursts into our home like an unexpected guest.

I always liked it when guests showed up unannounced—we were completely different that way. My whole life, I longed for a surprise party, but nobody ever organized one for me—at a certain point, you and everybody else started telling me it was impossible because I wanted it so badly. "It wouldn't be a surprise anymore, you know?" No, I didn't know. Christmas didn't stop being a surprise just because I knew it was coming. I dreamed that one day all of you would summon me to a beachside restaurant where all my friends and lovers would be waiting, surrounded by white roses and colorful balloons, with a piano and Pascoal's guitar, greeting me with the glorious sound of "The Shadow of the Clouds on the Sea."

God doesn't have a particular knack for music—while she may have tuned the strings of a few birds, certain types of rain, and ocean waves, she left the sublimity of sound to men. I always had the impression that God was a woman—and her lack of talent for music, judging by a statistical analysis of the great composers' genders, proves it. Further evidence still is her compassion for how much I miss you—which is also a kind of malice, of course, but no less compassionate for all that. I miss music, wish I could dance by your side in this nolus I'm drifting in. I did have my surprise party in the end—everybody showed up, flowers in hand, beside my coffin. But you're the only one who sang, pressed against the ice of my blue mouth.

36

Maybe paradise is all damp lawns and leafy trees full of squirrels, like Cambridge. We had a lot of fun at that stuffy conference on colonialism. There were a few dickheads who attended to show off not essays or research, but their prison stints, the torture they'd survived, as if these were medals recognizing human superiority. War taught me to be very dubious of guys who brag about things like that—heroes, at least the ones I've met, aren't big talkers (which, by the way, doesn't bode well for your career in heaven).

You got me into a right old mess during that conference. One night you came and banged on my door, claiming to be scared of a family of cockroaches or something like that. You knocked right as I was deepening my knowledge of Australian colonialism via the cutting-edge method of participatory research, between the sheets, with a highly skilled anthropologist. As soon as she heard your voice, the young woman pulled on her dress and leaped out the window— fortunately, my room was on the ground floor. Unfortunately, in the days that followed, I wasn't able to convince her you were just my best friend.

You didn't notice a thing, of course. Other people's indulgences tended to whiz right by you. Plus, though I never intended to hide my interest in the Australian from you, I didn't tell you anything about her. I found your obliviousness amusing. And to be honest, I was also afraid of your matchmaking efforts, which tended to bear a striking resemblance to a runaway train. Ultimately, I adopted the attitude of La Fontaine's fox, deciding that if those grapes weren't going to end up in my mouth, they must be sour.

I can't say I much enjoyed sleeping with my arms around you that night. But I think I faked it pretty well: I was the supportive friend you needed. We told each other stories, I tickled you, and I stroked your hair till you fell asleep. I slept very little that night, but good friends have to make these little sacrifices. Besides, *sacrifice* is a word created to describe the sadness of nonbelievers like me. Whereas you believed so very much.

37

We returned to Cambridge together on a future time curve. No conference-goers or English cocktails now—we were there to collaborate in writing our Alternative History of the World, a history in which original sin would be swapped out for the intelligence of love, and the Greek gods who inspired Dr. Freud would die once and for all, choked with guilt, after killing their fathers and sleeping with their mothers. A history in which the joy of discovery would fill the space occupied by destructive wars in the histories we'd heretofore been given.

We laughed so hard in that session on history and colonialism, remember? One of the panelists was a Bulgarian woman who'd been drinking the dregs from everybody's wineglasses and scarfing down leftovers after lunch. Then she started feeling sick. By the time she started reading her paper, her guts were on fire. As it happened, you were sitting next to her at the table. Flushed, she asked you to read the rest of the paper while she shoved her chair back and put her head between her knees. And so, in shaky English, you read her text, an inane treatise on the historical repression of women, dressed up in academic jargon. I bit my lip hard to keep from laughing, and you didn't dare even look over at me.

Other conference-goers wore prison sentences and censorship like medals— generally those whose experiences of imprisonment and humiliation were least significant. They often rounded out their presentations with bombastic readings of their unknown literary works—a poem, a poetic meditation, a story project in which the image "free as a bird" inevitably appeared as a sort of refrain.

I remember this French girl raising her hand to ask one of the ornithologists why he insisted on using such a tired metaphor. He responded gravely, "When you're in prison, you don't think in metaphors. The only thing I could see through my cell bars was a bird perched on a branch. I wanted to be as free as a bird." At that point, the two of us exchanged glances and fled—like birds ourselves—to go out riding bikes, punting on the autumnal Cam that flows behind the colleges, treasure hunting in the used bookstores.

I remember that night we shared a bed, stifling our laughter under the blankets so as not to draw attention to ourselves. I'd been reading in my peaceful bedroom when I saw a fat, hairy-legged spider walking across the bedsheet straight toward my nose. I killed it with the book, but, concerned about the whereabouts of Madam Spider's family abode, I went downstairs and knocked on your door. I crossed paths with a respectable Japanese professor in the hallway, and the next morning, the whispers had started up. We were twelve years old, or a hundred, and all we wanted was to talk nonsense, unfurling the static night of childhood over time until time disappeared.

37

Why is it that, whenever I leave the city, you feel farther away? They say the dead still echo in that derelict cavern known as the heart. That you can hear them in the silence, in the quietude of deserted places, in places like this, where it's possible to hear the involuntary muscle beating. But you were always a crowd. Your walled arrogance was always forgiven because a crowd swirled on the other side of those walls. Clinking wineglasses, piano music, muffled words, cigarette smoke. And books, books you devoured as eagerly as a lioness. "You read so much you end up not learning anything," I used to tell you. That was the kind of statement that cut you deepest. You didn't respond, afraid it might be true.

I no longer recall who it was who once called you a coin-operated chatterbox. You kept quiet the rest of the night, your eyes wet. If somebody called you selfish, nosy, vain, befuddled, you'd snap back with exquisite, triumphant wit. But we couldn't touch the small black keys of your grand piano. The music was gone.

Where has my music gone? I open the window, letting the noise of the night city rush in, and put on your music. The music of that slovenly vagrant whose death you grieved so keenly, the music of Paris that we both loved so much and so independently. I light a cigar and sit waiting for you, waiting for a sign from that other clochard who took you away from me without giving me time to discover who you were.

38

Messing up your books. I'd like to have the force of a gust of air so I could at least knock the one at the top of the pile out of place. Everything was always in order, even in the weekend home we ended up sharing. I was obsessed with internal organization—alphabetical, topical—while you were more concerned with external harmony: the spines had to proceed in a chromatic sequence, chaos presenting the appearance of serenity.

Our weekend home: white with blue trim. With an overgrown garden that you tamed by force—the grass refused to take hold, the palm tree to grow. Inside the windows, stone benches where a person could spend days staring out at the sea. You hated the damp, the musty smell in your clothing, the gray blotches on the walls, the mold on your shoes. I liked wearing clothing that was mildewed and stale—it made me feel at peace. Remote from the urban world that was, that still is, my drug.

Cities feel feverish, like teenagers, dancing on the trails of their own light, consumed by a diffuse unease, cruel, free, impure, lovers of newness, with all their inaugural filth. Places of waiting and construction, levity and levitation, where events unfold in a chained sequence and the tiny truth of each truly exists, altering the chemical composition of the whole at every turn. You sometimes used to say that cities are exhausting in their soullessness. Darling, smog is composed of the bluish ballast of souls, ancient and future souls struggling to infiltrate the flesh of the present, to turn memory into a house under construction. Souls frayed by what they have been unable to achieve—cities give us the measure of the unattainable, which is why we can't manage to rid ourselves of them.

There's always a glimmer of death on any corner of the cities we love, the footsteps of someone who no longer exists but still walks before us, the sound of their steps mingling with the steps of those who are yet to be born. There's a lack of silence, of resignation to death, in cities—I refuse to resign myself; I can't sleep in peace, can't give up this urban whirlwind marked by my wheezing breath.

Red carnations are bleeding against the white of your walls. You always preferred roses, or else camellias. You used to make fun of my carnation obsession, and now there you are, surrounded by them, in that teal tank top I gave you that you never wore because you thought it was garish. You're wearing the teal tank top, lying on the pale wooden planks of your unruffled house. The books all around you, murmuring armies in formation. The carnations, the green, the Gainsbourg song ("How can you be so fond of a man who bathes so little and shaves so sloppily?" you used to ask)—it seems that I had to die to be able to enter your house.

38

I hang on to too many dead from the past. Stupid dead, their guts hanging out, eyes wide, lost on their way to the other world. War dead, kids who died screaming for their mothers or for girlfriends whose scent they'd barely gotten to know. Dead who make my sleep and my dreams founder. For years they've been floating inside my body; for years I've been removing them with an eyedropper and transferring them to my memory so they don't get contaminated with my life.

We rejected the rituals of death because they interfered with the supposed asceticism of mourning. And we stayed like that, awash in bodies stinking in the caverns of our hearts. We can't cleanse our hearts like they do in your Russian classics: remorse and guilt, which scrubbed our souls as efficiently as bleach for so many centuries, are out of fashion. As are cries of pain, impassioned confessions, the incomplete fury of human suffering.

The dead these days autopsy themselves, cut themselves open and sew themselves up again, eulogize themselves, mourn themselves, bury themselves. Wakes are therapy sessions, and the only therapeutic modality is forgetting. If the deceased's mother or father or son wants to talk all night about the light of that dead smile, then a phalanx of friends descends to propose an endless series of distractions, hushing the bereaved and urging them away from the body that—in extremely poor taste—they're trying to kiss and hug and warm with the scalding liquid of their tears. The dead have become mannequins—things to be dressed and undressed, assembled and disassembled, fodder for erotic theories, for audiences and statistics, the regressive refuge of loners who make of necrology a transdisciplinary art form. The dead are photographed en masse when they die en masse, rather than in the individual modesty of power and money. Or they are produced in life, at the hands of a platoon of makeup artists, following the instructions of visual artists seeking to say the unsayable. We tinker with the dead more and more all the time.

When Alexandre's wife died, he sat with her body for two days and two nights, kissing her, bathing her with tears, taking photos of her. He photographed her in bed and in her coffin, bald and gaunt as a Holocaust victim. Everybody whispered about how tacky it was. They tried to dissuade him with their litany of distractions, but he shook off the comfort vultures, even the priests, in one fell swoop: "If you all want to eat dinner, sleep, or get some rest, please go do it on your own—leave me the fuck alone!"

I wish I'd cursed like that at your coffin. So much whispering about your pregnancy, so much putrid prying into the father of that deadly child, so much Mexican soap opera sullying the air of that room redolent with your body's last presence. *Leave me the fuck alone, damn it,* I thought with such intensity that I saw a smile flicker across your pallid face. You winked at me and said, "Let them entertain themselves with their mental fuckery. They don't have the imagination for any other kind, poor things." Death may have made you merciful, but it didn't crush your wit.

I wish I'd had the courage to affront good manners. To keep a photo of you looking like that, white and caustic. Truly dead, in old-fangled silence. I needed that photograph so I could imagine you growing old serenely, free myself of the weight of the dreams you never fulfilled. But you replaced the practical sense of dreams with the prophetic state of ideas a long time ago. That pursuit of the impossible made your life run faster. Yes, you were killing yourself in life too. Absolutely. You knew everything there is to know. You experienced the full range of passions, marvels, and disappointments. You were older than me by the time you died. I envy you the swiftness and unpredictability of your death—can you arrange one like that for me too, or does everybody die at the pace they lived? Because if that's the case, Tink, I'm screwed. Unless I can learn to be quick and efficient. But first I have to figure out how the sun can be shining down so yellowly brazen on a world that no longer has you in it.

39

Don't let me die. Give me an eternal space in your mortal body. I don't want you to come to me; the dead never meet—maybe they all wander around here, in the black pits of time, watching over the living who never were able to love, even at the end. Maybe only love has no end—their love wounded, red and black; tattered, miserable, human love. Whenever I tried to love humanity, I ended up alone and angry, loving only myself—or feeling sorry for myself, which is basically the same thing. Pain is part of love, bolsters it over time. Like a red carnation, withered and forgotten. Every wilted carnation contains the concentrated past and future of all carnations.

I liked wrinkles so much—ironic, isn't it?—and I never ended up getting them. So many women lie in hospital beds, anesthetized, to awaken bandaged and numb, giving over days of their short lives to pain in order to free themselves from the marks of aging—and I, who loved the way time marks bodies, who dreamed of my lovers' future furrows, their bodies' fatigue, their souls' open wounds visible in their eyes, here I am, nowhere at all.

I can see the earth far below the clouds, but I'm not experiencing that blue tranquility I used to feel on airplanes. The houses would shrink beneath the wings carrying me, the cars like ants and human ambitions suddenly irrelevant. Now I am the wing, a feather's very essence—and only with you, my self-assured sexagenarian, am I able to rest.

If I move away from you, I hear shouts, a chorus of shouts coming from I know not where; the earth goes out of focus and I collapse in an agonizing inconsistency—which, you'd point out with a cackle, neatly sums up my life.

But your laughter seems to have died with me—go on, laugh, throw your arms in the air and laugh wildly, the way you always laughed at me. Want to know a secret? The world doesn't make sense—and I'm still here, who knows where, waiting for something to happen. Women never get tired of waiting for something to happen, you'd say, which is why they don't age as quickly. Or, rather, are born old.

To be born again, have a space to tread, feel my breath on one of Lisbon's high, long windows—space exists only insofar as it is reduced to the measure of a body, to the glow of flesh. Was I beautiful enough that my presence can remain, illuminating the void I once filled? Was any void ever mine?

The weight of the world. If only I could touch a child's face for a moment to stanch it, to regain the illusion that such a thing might be possible, to close the doors of pain, torture, injustice. Drive them into that black hole somewhere in outer space. I try to take you by the hand; I take the cold hand of my mother who never died. Hold my hand, Mother—why do your fingers refuse to grasp mine? I was angry with my mother when she died—were you angry with me too? Is that why you never laugh?

Why don't you answer the phone? The world is calling you—a world of opportunists and opportunities. Of dead children and people who write poems about dead children. Of life that isn't stanched in the screams of the children who, at this very moment, are being tortured by their mothers. While you listen to St. Matthew Passion and think sorrowfully of me, I think sorrowfully of you while listening to the futile weeping of a little girl whose mother is burning her with an iron. My whole life, I always heard these children's cries—because I didn't have children, because I pretty much didn't have parents, because we're all orphans. We do odd jobs, struggle to survive, perform theater pieces with the roles reversed. I served as your mother so many times, watched you pasting my smile onto your memories of the miserable mother fate stuck you with. You fell asleep with your head on my lap so many times, elderly son of my own choosing. Pick up the phone, Son. The flotsam of what we used to call "our group" is looking for you.

39

Our friends keep calling me. They say I need to react, tell me to write. To write you. You stay my hand. You don't want me to write you. You don't want me to make anything new, anything that alters our history. We planned to write texts fifty-fifty. We set ground rules: we'd steal from each other. But we didn't write to each other much. We didn't need that artifice of explanatory seduction. And we definitely don't need it now. I find you with open eyes—in the voids of silence in my house, in the interstices of evening crowds, in the fog of my breath on the windows when cold crushes the night.

In those first days, I was afraid of gradually forgetting you, but it's not true what people say about time. God may snatch life away from us—yes, the Big Dude's easy to point the finger at—but he doesn't see details. And sanding down time is a matter of focusing on details. Instead of allowing that punk-ass God of yours to keep me down with your irreversible disappearance and our irrevocable mistakes, I pretend that you never existed. I invent you as my own creation, the realest of imaginary friends. I shake you free of time, make you my friend before and after the chronology you were given.

You appear one Christmas Eve, after dinner, with your parents. A huge pink ribbon, almost bigger than your head, hasn't been able to tame your rebellious curls. There's no sparkle in your mother's eyes, which are light in color but dim, and maybe that's why your noisy laugh stands out so much—as if only that laugh could bring these three people together.

Your parents' car has broken down in front of our house, and they ask to use the phone. But luckily there is no mechanic available to pick up the family and take you away on this Christmas Eve in 1943. My mother invites you to stay—what difference would another three people make in a house full of aunts and uncles and cousins? We're both six years old and devoutly believe that the Baby Jesus is going to come down the chimney at daybreak to fill our shoes with toys.

My cousins and siblings and I have been preparing a skit to make the long wait pass more cheerfully. It's a religion-themed detective piece: somebody has stolen the Wise Men's gold, incense, and myrrh. Saint Joseph, in what I believe must be the only star turn he's ever enjoyed, is our Sherlock Holmes. You immediately come up with three songs to weave the story together, insisting that every play needs musical numbers. All of them have the same melody (the classic "Silent Night"), but you say the important part is the lyrics. Even back then, you always get the last word, and I immediately dislike you. You refuse to play the Virgin Mary and write a new part for yourself. In the end, you play Saint Joseph's assistant, a gossipy shepherdess who discovers it was one of the Baby Jesus's angel friends who stole the gold to buy shoes for all the barefoot children in the world. The adults clap, we pass a hat as their applause dies down, and only my grandfather refuses to pay up: "Money doesn't buy happiness, kids." My grandmother pays double, behind his back, with coins filched from the household budget, which she's been bilking her entire married life.

The fireplace from that night of my childhood crackles in my flameless fireplace. I see the two of us watching the logs burning on that magical night of our shared youth. Later, when everybody is sleeping, we sit on the stairs that lead up to the bedrooms, waiting to see the Baby Jesus come down the chimney with our bag of gifts. "Does he somehow know I'm at your house?" you ask me. Yes, he knows.

40

If only I could go sit on the stairs of the lover who humiliated me. Feel my heart pounding in my throat, the insolent terror of passion. Because in the end I loved one man, just one, the way I loved God—with the desperate certainty that he was the one and that I'd never be able to live with him. I lost the privilege of disillusionment. If I were alive again, dear friend, I'd go track down that man I criticized to you so harshly, and I'd eagerly embrace the brutal love I wasn't seeking. The brutal love that belongs only to the places of life, the chemistry of bodies. I can't return to the darkness of time, the darkness of his stairs, on tiptoe.

Light under the crack of the door, hours spent trying to identify his footsteps, trying to suss out whether the voices in the house were issuing from the fifth dimension offered by mass communication devices or were right there, on the other side of the door, ready to pounce on the brutality of my love. I'd sit for hours there in the dark, at the cliff's edge, drawing strength from the drumbeat of the rain falling on the skylight. I went there most of all on rainy nights—it was like storms dragged me out of the house, my eyes swamped with tears that turned the city into an intoxication of light. Afterward, sometimes, I'd knock, hoping that surprise might reveal on his face the image of his love for me.

40

I bump into you again beneath a tunnel of cedars sometime in the late sixties. I've only recently returned from Africa, and Alexandre has rebuilt a tumbledown house he inherited and invited me to visit. Fall is at the peak of its golden splendor. Alexandre has extended the house to span the stream that flows past it, and the music of the tumbling water pervades the silence of the rooms, which are all granite and pale wood, sketched at disjointed angles. A few yards from the front door, a staircase shaded by a dense tunnel of cedars leads to the vineyards, which, at this time of year, glow like steady flames.

I'm climbing the stairs toward the house when I see you coming down, holding hands with a man whose features I don't even register. You're wearing a long-sleeved green-and-pink dress, a pink knitted coat over your shoulders, and the same remarkable pink ribbon in your curls, which are now long. You smile at me and say, "I can't stay with you now, it's not time yet." When I turn to get a better look, you've already disappeared. I search, but there's no sign of you or the mysterious man in the vineyard. Not even in the stand of trees on the far side. I ask Alexandre who the strange couple could have been, and he insists that we're alone here—me, him, and his wife.

And I never think about that encounter again until the day I see you standing in front of me in that history class, a completely inadequate (and crooked) blue ribbon tied in your black curls. But of course you can't be the little girl or the young woman I remember. Unless you're the female reincarnation of Peter Pan. In which case your death makes no sense. I feel the light of your smile in tiny lacerations on my skin. I know you're here—but why don't you talk to me?

41

You never liked groups anyway. "Herds are the worst!" you always said. But you were so theatrical in saying it. I eventually came to see it as a cry for help. The world was one long SOS, and I loved it—you were right about that. Now that I was no longer writing books or sculpting statues, at least I was leaving my mark on other people's happiness. I'd seen the world that could be saved. Even, or especially, the people who didn't want to be saved.

What did I save you from, though? You were a staunch loner when I met you, and even more solitary when I left. You started out as what Musil would call a "man of the real," apt to inflame the possibilities hidden in the folds of reality. You eventually slid into the Musilian territory of the "man of the possible," for whom everything that exists, visible and invisible alike, has the same weight. And that made you an impossible man—lighter than a leaf on the wind, the infinite leaf that every autumn returns on the wind of mutant cities.

You became addicted to my laughter, addicted even to those happy herds I dragged along with me from the movies to the theater, from the theater to the cafés. Fish Stick and Silver Tongue. Joana the Mad (whose name wasn't even Joana) and the Three Little Pigs, always whining about the wolves that ruined all their endeavors. None of them were aware of their nicknames.

When you ran into the group of us eating dinner at the seaside one summer night, you tossed me a wry smile: "So the whole zoo's here, then. All that's missing is the old gorilla—and here I am." You rebuffed my timid invitation for you to sit with us, saying you didn't have the patience for political discussions or stories about people's kids, which would ultimately lead to the same place. One of the Three Little Pigs had recently become a father, and I don't think he appreciated the direct allusion to the presence of his newborn son. But it was actually me you were talking about—or was that just me feeling more important than I was? I wanted to change the world, and yes, our friends sought me out because they wanted better jobs. And I truly believed that what they wanted was to help me change the world. At least at first. There was a precise chronological coincidence between my party's decline in the polls and the intensifying silence of my answering machine. But it was only months later that I made that connection.

When the Three Little Pigs finally managed to start the art history magazine they'd been dreaming of, they called you, not me. And you, you bastard, wrote a perfect essay about my beloved Georgia O'Keeffe. With all the best ideas from my classes you'd attended. And you started your radio career by expressing your gratitude to the Three Little Pigs, talking about your long-standing friendship as if it had been born thanks to the efforts and grace of the Holy Spirit.

How you fumed about those Little Pig bastards at first. One because he was always bumming other people's cigarettes, another because he always ordered the last crème brûlée at restaurants, and the third because he always had to have the last word. Anyway. You dog. Ugly, angry, rabid dog. Let me tell you everything, now that I can't tell you anything. I couldn't see you the way the others did, so I spent my life erasing from the tape any scene that would ruin my vision of you. I stopped calling you so I could love you like I used to, pretend you'd become invisible but were still by my side. Toothless dog. It's only now that you're missing me. When I couldn't believe in you as an invisible friend, I imagined you ailing, deathly ill, fetid. The elegant perfume of cigars in your house replaced by the infectious stench of illness—and you, at death's door, revived when you heard my name. God exists, don't you see? He took revenge on me for that Camillian fantasy.

Look, that robe I bought you—do you remember that was me? You got sick for real once—not terribly sick, just enough to start yelping for me. I never met a man who dared fight off an illness without some kind of stand-in maternal figure. You'd stopped phoning me every day by that point. Your voice weak, you begged me to go out and buy you a warm robe before the flu consumed the heat of your life force. You'd only just realized you didn't have one. You never wore one, even in winter. And so I went off on that rainy April afternoon to find a robe made of pure wool (as specified), preferably in a blue-and-green tartan.

It took me three hours to track one down—the stores weren't selling anything but warm-weather clothing—but I managed it. And then I crossed the city in the opposite direction, on my own initiative, to buy you some fresh-baked puff pastries, oranges from the Algarve, and Bravo de Esmolfe apples—because you refused to eat any other kind. But I'd forgotten to bring the key to your house.

I knocked on the door, and a friend I'd never seen before answered. A man nearly your age, but even taller and almost better looking. I immediately considered him a friend; being so taken with you, I naturally believed that all of your friends were part of you. A tendency left over from my high school days, afternoons spent sitting on stairs with my fingers twined in my best friend's blond hair and my head on the shoulder of a boy who liked her. But my brand-new friend eyed me suspiciously and told me you couldn't see me because you were sick. I smiled again, displayed my treasures, explained that I was there to take care of you, and ducked into the house beneath the closed gate of his arm.

You complained about the color of the robe (which was blue-and-black plaid instead of blue-and-green) and about how the pastries had gotten cold. You whined about how long I'd taken and kept arguing with your friend about all the different interpretations of Bach. Afterward you sent me flowers with a brief note of apology. But I didn't want your flowers. It's not like I was dead.

41

Maybe it was the disease of eternity, which always ends up infecting history lovers—even the ironic types, like us—that knocked our clocks out of sync. You were still attempting to show up on time to your scheduled obligations. You gave it your all and almost pulled it off. You'd noticed that punctual people tended to be respected. And respect was something you were obsessed with. Respect is one of the traps women stumble into. If you were looking to subvert the world's chauvinistic order, wouldn't it have been better to start by disrupting the way time is regimented? That time you threw a public fit in front of the TV cameras because you'd arrived at Parliament too late to vote on the priority-setting bill, wouldn't it have been better to give a dignified, disdainful shrug instead of babbling excuses?

Somehow you managed to appear to me before you'd even been born, kid. You were generally even less punctual than me because you always had an endless list of things to do and refused to accept the finitude of each hour. You lacked war experience. Just as I lack experience with the guerilla warfare of the day-to-day, darning this and patching that, the struggle to endure that wards off the smell of death.

I'm an old man—and already was when we met. But you never noticed that. I tire easily. If it weren't for my young criminals' thirst for knowledge, I wouldn't be interested in anything at this point. My body is retreating from me—it hardly ever responds to my concerns, slides toward the earth's horizon. I was afraid my skin might start to smell stale, that my dentures would tumble into my soup. That you'd start showing up at my house just one Sunday a month, to find me sitting in a wheelchair, waiting for you to play cards with me. Old people my age emigrate, take up residence in anecdotes about that time when they were happy, in wartime forests or childhood games of marbles.

When you were alive, even in those final years when we were only the memory of what we used to be, I fed off the ups and downs of your life. The jokes, the sarcasm, the euphoric rage of seeing my muse trip on the false-bottomed staircase of power. I was so resolutely your friend that I was also your fiercest enemy—always expecting more and better from you. An asinine enemy who failed to keep you alive.

I wish I knew your killer's name. Something tells me it was that seraphic prowler for unwary women, like a dead gecko on sunny walls attracting a foolish fly. That bourgeois Adonis who seduced both you and that waifish Flor chick from the department. I don't remember seeing him at your funeral. Pascoal whispered something to me about an old flame, but I didn't listen, unwilling to accept that I was no longer your confidant.

But in matters of the heart, you were supremely predictable, practically meteorological. If a boyfriend dumped you, you'd move on to another so you could forget the first. Your outings were always returns to the past, and your men were just corpses in the making that you struggled to resuscitate. Your God gave you the soul of an undertaker. He probably called you away early so you could help him bring the dead there on the other side back to life. Now you've left me here with this ignominious detective work—waiting for death to come solve my case.

42

I am moved by your slumber. Who am I to find it moving? Your breathing in the green light of dawn. I open incandescences in your dreams—I always knew them better than you. Or at least I believed in them—in your capacity to be that dream. You are bereft of God. The limping God who created me, that God you roundly mock. Poor suffering atheist—excuse the redundancy. Go on and laugh—God is laughter. Since the world's initial explosion, he's never stopped laughing at his creation.

Look at you. Your body covered with white fuzz. Up close, you look like a charred forest. You're snoring—you don't exactly sound like Bach. Your mouth gaping, a thread of saliva dampening the pillow. Six white plastic teeth, plus a bunch of black ones. The loose flesh around your navel rising and falling to the sound of the hollow music of your slumber. Your tobacco-stained fingers, your eyes hidden behind sleep. Your bushy, crooked eyebrows. Your pleated elbows. Four large black moles around your nose. A bald spot on the back of your head. The pockmarked intimacy of your beauty.

You used to get mad when I'd leave around piles of old magazines that cluttered the living room. But you always left the bathroom littered with your hair from shaving. You'd say you were going to set the table and then sit down to read the newspaper. You'd say, "I'll be right down," and I'd wait in the taxi, watching the meter tick up, picturing you leisurely choosing a coat or flipping through the TV channels one last time.

The two of us really did live outside of time. We once arranged to meet for dinner next to the movie theater at eight, and we both showed up at the box office breathless and panting, simultaneously, at a quarter past nine. "I had a hard time being a soldier—I'm not cut out for military discipline," you'd say. If you didn't keep opening those photo albums, if you didn't reread my letters so many times, it would be hard for me to remember the rest of it, the immense rest of it that was our happiness.

The way we could sit in silence, reading side by side on warm Alentejan afternoons. Or recall the same phrase at the same time. Or, with the exchange of a single glance, communicate our opinions of somebody in the clearest terms. You used to identify everybody with characters from Eça de Queiroz's novels— Gouvarinho, or Pacheco, or Dâmaso, or João da Ega. Our constant laughter at other people's expense refreshed us most of all. We couldn't have been more Queirozian, lolling on our bellies and demanding the utmost excellence from our country. I wanted to escape from that impasse, and came to regret it. Public life wasn't the solution either—Eça's books could have told us that too.

42

Why is everybody trying to force me to be happy? They issue a series of warnings: if I don't leave the house, if I don't dispel the silence you've left me in, if I don't learn to forget, everybody will forget about me. I'll end up without any friends, without a cup of tea in the extended nighttime of modern old age, without the human warmth I never deserved. I don't give a crap about deserved warmth. Contrary to popular belief, friendship isn't something a person deserves.

Love is, though: we gain twenty pounds, lose our teeth, copulate a few dozen times, and there goes our love, sailing through the sky, off to greener pastures. Love is a matter of weights and dumbbells, feathers and kindlings—oh, how well I remember. A tedious hassle of flowers and poems, studied absences and enigmatic presences, an endless reenactment of the tale of Little Red Riding Hood. The decanted discoveries of love seemed to me to be nothing but gymnastics of the imagination. Bonus: when love fails, we get to blame it on fate—that circumspect bureaucrat in your God's employ. With alpaca-wool sleeve protectors and briefcases full of forms to be filled out in case of divorce: the books to me, the record collection to you, the dishware divided between us, and that's that. Fate files the paperwork and accepts the blame, our weakness shielded under the heavens, and sends down a few more cupids so the show can go on.

So all our mistakes pile up against the curved haunch of that vague, silent fate, now carved into a spiral's black aesthetic. We justify our mistakes in love by pointing to the senselessness that provokes them—as if love didn't always burgeon and then subside on the basis of the color of a pair of eyes, the curve of a waist, the specific chemistry of sex. Any additional mistakes are attributed to friendship. They spread across the world in geographies of sharing or antagonism. And we justify them by humans' inability to perceive things clearly in a universe that's been forsaken by the gods, that is awash in chaos. We end up thinking our mistakes are destiny. Such a notion leads to places where good conscience and deficient willpower conspire to keep us immobile in the face of enormous atrocities. But who's willing to subject himself to endless talk of good and evil, who's willing to commit to someone else's flaws and characteristics till death do they part, merely in exchange for that vast void known as friendship?

Why did I choose you? Why was I always at your side? Because both of us believed in the transformative power of each human being on this earth. That fundamental ethical choice pushed us toward each other. But the endurance of that choice through the unfortunate happenstances of daily life—that's what I can't explain. Being born on the same side of the bridge of our fundamental choices doesn't explain everything. Because there is, despite everything, a multitude around us. There is a multitude of chorusing voices in every arena of the ethics by which we choose our friends. I chose you, yes, because of one or two core affinities—but affinities don't tell the whole story.

If you'd ever started defending dictatorships, erasing faces from photos, or relativizing the value of freedom, I wouldn't have been able to keep calling you my friend. And even then, I'd attempt to garb your transformation in the mantle of illness, find a psychiatrist who could treat you—and I don't believe in psychiatry! But if you killed, betrayed, or stole without renouncing our fundamental credo, I would swear, my eyes swimming with tears, to your innocence.

In Africa, I saw plenty of incorruptible men commit crimes out of fear, throwing bombs with their backs turned to death, buying women because faraway girlfriends had fallen silent. And those very same men hurled themselves in front of younger soldiers to protect us during ambushes. Or ran into burning huts because they heard screaming. I saw how brightly human goodness shone amid the horror it created. I saw the shit I'm made of in that moment when I paused to rest and my platoon-mate set off the land mine that should have been for me.

I also saw betrayal after the war, carried out in cold blood, in the most routine way. During the transition to democracy known as the Ongoing Revolutionary Process, for example, the father of one of my comrades died. That father, whom I never met, was apparently an obscure defender of Marcelo Caetano, the last leader of the authoritarian Estado Novo. Standing next to the coffin, the son harshly criticized his father, pointing out his failures and amplifying his faults. The political comrades of my brother-in-arms applauded what they called impartial justice and what sounded to me like ingratitude. So I turned away, at the end of that funeral and for good, from ongoing revolutionaries—who swiftly changed tracks anyway so they could snag the best seats on the trains of the counterrevolution. I know you were next to me in that cemetery at the moment when, beneath a punishing sun, I allowed my comrade to insult the father who was sinking into the earth.

I know you were next to me, even though you were just thirteen and I'd already entered midlife—like your parents, whose death was looming. I picture you, a piece of chewing gum in your mouth, playing tag with other kids your age—and you were already my friend.

It's hard not to get to see you grow old, hard not to be able to tell you that I'd love you exactly the same. Toothless, addled, wrinkled—my friend. A woman born with the exact right amount of laughter in her. My accomplice, even against the two of us. I never loved another woman like that. You got a little greedy, a little tipsy on the champagne of power, but you never fell into the vicious circle of bad faith. You were able to preserve that innocence through which sincere volition is able to achieve the impossible.

43

If I hadn't been so caught up in what you called public life, maybe I'd have noticed the new self that was being born in the wrong place inside me. I never realized I was pregnant—the pregnant women I'd known talked about other kinds of symptoms: an uncomfortable mix of overwhelming nausea and sudden cravings.

Some of them, the spiritual types, swore they could tell they were pregnant as soon as they conceived. They claimed child-producing orgasms had a special quality to them. I was dumbstruck by their belief in the fecund power of pleasure. If that were really the case, how did humanity reproduce before the twentieth century, in eras when the female orgasm was a heresy—or, in the most generous interpretation, a well-guarded secret? Plus, had it been the case, I'd have had a house full of children.

But these philosophers of intuition talked about an immediate inner peace, an instantaneous wisdom that guided them to the uterus as soon as the task was completed. Needless to say, I didn't put a lot of stock in it. I'm sure you'll remember Lígia, my colleague in the sociology department, who practiced tarot and Reiki, declared herself an absolute pacifist, and spent her life trying to educate me. She thought I was too competitive, insisted that I was wasting my "psychic gifts," that I was being carried along by ignorant pragmatism. She once got really upset with me because I told her during a public debate that I was grateful to the English for not offering Hitler their other cheek. In her view, if we refused to respond to aggressors' attacks, the universe would be plunged into perpetual harmony.

But when her husband traded her in for another woman ninety pounds of pacifism lighter, that angel of kindness hired a bulldog of a lawyer to extort him for all he was worth. For the good of the children, naturally—two boys, eight and ten, who showed up at court in tears to confirm their father's betrayal. She got mad at me because I refused to testify against the cheater—and, ever the pragmatist, I seized the opportunity to tell her what I thought of mothers who turned their children against their fathers. You always said I didn't know how to get along, that I shouldn't say everything I thought out loud—but you loved me, still love me, for my relentless disregard for those and other niceties.

I got pregnant pragmatically too, and I didn't even realize it. A week before I died, I felt sharp pains in my belly, but I didn't connect the dots. I took deep breaths and figured it was just a product of the stress I was under because all my projects seemed fated to languish and die under my parliamentary coalition's insistent neglect.

It was the beginning of March, Women's History Month, when politicians and journalists rediscover a mostly dormant interest in women for a few weeks, and I received a number of invitations from different cities to give a talk on the status of Portuguese women. I accepted them all. I took particular delight in accepting invitations from municipalities run by other political parties. I was determined to prove that I wasn't just valuable as a party-line vote, as my peers obviously believed. So I ignored the sudden pangs gnawing at my entrails like wolves.

Two days before I died, I started bleeding—but I was in a remote part of Beira and figured I'd just go to the doctor when I got back to Lisbon. I also felt vaguely guilty because Pascoal, who'd been my friend since high school, had wanted to meet up before I left on my tour, and I'd put him off. Now I hadn't seen him in six months, and our reunion was going to have to wait another month. He told me he'd split up with Augusto, but that wasn't what he wanted to talk about.

How is it that I couldn't bring myself to call off a lecture that ended up being attended by half a dozen women, more as a break from their rural solitude than for any other reason, and rush to the aid of a friend going through an emotional crisis? What was I becoming? I believed, you see, that those agonizing stabs of pain were a punishment from God. I preferred the vanity of friendship—however much I hid that fact with the velvety kindnesses of altruism, it was the truth.

Pascoal called again, an unaccustomed agitation in his voice; I was somewhere in Ribatejo. "Come on, ditch that crap. I really need you here. Are you sure you're OK?" Not wanting him to worry, I didn't tell him about the pain. I figured I had an ectopic pregnancy. I knew what an ectopic pregnancy was.

No, it wasn't your fault, Pascoal. Can anyone be at fault for what never comes to pass? Whose fault was the flood of desire that drew me to the skin enfolding the lover who was never actually mine? Whose fault was that carnivorous intimacy that pushed us toward the silence of pleasure before we even met? Maybe it was our neglect of the body that was to blame.

We met at Frágil; I must have been twenty and he twenty-eight, and we were pretty much the only ones there who weren't dancing. I found them ridiculous, all those peacocks with their exaggeratedly sexual movements. Maybe I wasn't being fair—we rarely are when we join the frieze of clinical observers. But I couldn't imagine living as a mere testimony to my own body, adopting a corporal lifestyle of vigorous, gymnastic health, rituals of dress and movement— in other words, I was completely unfashionable. As was he, hunched over the bar, drinking and smoking cigarette after cigarette, watching. We hardly spoke. My eyes were held captive by his mouth. Large, fleshy lips, almost obscenely motionless. The flirtatious conversations around the bar provoked a faint smile on his face that was reflected identically on mine.

I went back to Frágil a week later. The third week, I followed him out as he was leaving. Only when I woke up the next morning did he ask, "What's your name?"

I told him I didn't know anymore. That's the sort of thing you say only at twenty, even if it continues to be true. He immediately told me his full name, as a warning. We couldn't pretend to be lost. Perdition was written in his blood, but not in his life. He took off and left me there in bed.

At fifteen I used to dream of the day when I'd lose all fear, claim possession of immense clarity. That's how adults seemed to me—people who weren't afraid of the dentist, didn't have to pass exams, and had no trouble sniffing out romantic fakery. Ultimately, that day didn't exist. Darkness grows with us—the only difference is that some people eventually realize that nothing matters, or they come to consider all love the finite progeny of a boundless fraud.

That wasn't the case with me—God refused to let my heart rest. As a child, I was never able to see clouds in the clouds and grass in the grass. I couldn't help questioning first principles and still can't separate the parts from the whole. He took off and left me in bed, the man that God sent to kill me. We met up like that for the rest of my life. When I couldn't find him, I'd wait on his doorstep—he lived in an attic apartment, so it was impossible to tell when he was home.

The first time, he enjoyed the surprise. The first time, he found me sitting on the stairs, which was actually the tenth time I'd been there, waiting on the dark street, with my feet frozen and a desperate joy like that of a child in danger. He laughed, stroked my face, took my hand, and led me up the stairs. The second time, his brow furrowed chidingly, but his eyes were still laughing. He didn't take my hand, but he invited me up. The third time, he turned on his heel and went to hail a cab on the next block. Between the second and third times, I'd committed a fatal error: I'd introduced him to some friends of mine at Frágil. He fled after the introductions. So I gave up on him.

Three months later we ran into each other at the entrance to the university. He told me the friend he'd come to see was out and took me for coffee. We'd always get to this point where I'd attempt to become part of his everyday life, and he'd back away. I'd pound on the door of his house. And I'd pound on him too, sometimes. I left him for good four or five times. I don't know how he always managed to run into me right as my normal relationships were entering that most excruciatingly normal phase of all—death.

One night I walked into Frágil and he was pouring that toxic smile of his onto Florbela, a nice girl whom God gave an immersion blender instead of a brain, probably to make her life as soft as mashed potatoes. To little avail—God likes fooling himself too, otherwise he wouldn't have constructed a world that is a spiral of deceptions to relieve our boredom.

Simple Florbela was always moaning about how complicated life was. She found everything complex: faucets, relationships, computers, the lunch menu, the simplest conversation. You'd ask her if she was OK, and she'd furrow her brow as she weighed the question. There were only two certainties lurking behind that furrowed brow: that she was pretty and that men, in general, liked sleeping with her. But even those certainties were disjointed, disconnected. I knew Florbela well because she was the secretary in my department. I joined her for a lot of fruit salads, her primary food group. She was always either really, really in love or really, really distraught—and sometimes the two conditions overlapped, which was really, really complicated for Florbela. She'd appear, pleading, over my shoulder: "Would you like to come eat a salad with me?"

The morning after that night I saw her emerge, smitten, with my lover, lovely Flor dragged me out for one of her urgent salads. She told me how my lover had spent hours kissing her fingers, one by one, with the slowest, wettest tongue in the solar system. She told me about all the positions he'd put her in, how many times he'd set her on fire, and how long each of his ecstasies lasted. She felled an entire forest of details and then finished it off, swelling with radiant pride, the silicone of her breasts ready to burst under her low-cut blouse, licking her bowl—she always licked the bowl when she finished her salad:

"And he's coming, he's coming by the university to see me this afternoon."

What a pig. Rotten hunk of apple—who did he think he was poisoning? And me there, so intelligent, so kind, so learned, nurturing the cheerful passions of the fairy Florbela, who had a blender for a brain and had turned the most interesting challenge of my life into mashed potatoes. That afternoon, I didn't teach my classes. I said I wasn't feeling well, and Florbela pouted: she'd wanted to introduce her boyfriend. I never told you this—it would have been too humiliating to repeat it, even to my other half. You knew Florbela, and I was afraid you'd stop liking me if you knew that we'd fallen for the same guy. And that, to top it off, he'd preferred scrawny Florbela. I imagined your wicked laugh ascending the folds of a resolute disdain. Besides, I was too sad.

I never figured out how to put the brakes on sadness. I died many times to keep from dying. I still find in sadness the comforting whiff of life. I no longer know what it means to be cold or hot or hurting—but I'm still sad, therefore I exist. I need to work the oil paints of my mortal sadnesses to achieve an abstract melancholy. I need that abstraction to fill your pores—I need to inhabit you, shape you, my baroque cubist heart. Sadness prevents me from finishing dying—here, Prof, let your blood accommodate the immodest modesty of what used to be me. Remembering my contours isn't enough—take the childish nonsense I never gave you, tears discolored by the fingerprints of my chocolate heart. Eat them, let me die inside you—let me choose to die inside you, because death is the only thing I lack.

Having been suddenly reduced to a teenage reject at the peak of my academic career, I had to stop seeing Florbela. Believe it or not, that's another reason I went into politics: because I'd been unwittingly humiliated by a sweet simpleton. The glory of God doesn't scorn the least-charted routes—and he takes no pleasure from people invoking the divine or, as we called it, the masses, which is the same thing. I spent less and less time at the university. I claimed I worked better at home, in silence. I stopped going to that nightclub. And four years passed.

I only saw him again a few months before I died, at one of those fundraising galas for AIDS victims. I pretended not to have seen him, and he came up to me, smiling, his hand extended: "You wouldn't refuse a handshake to a humble constituent, would you?" Son of a bitch, my A side growled in my core. Meanwhile, my B side had already started barking: Who does this bastard think he is? Why is fate putting this lowlife at my table? Did he come here on purpose to see me? Later, my survival instinct persuaded me that this generous servicer of Florbela's, deep, deep down, had been born to bring me back to life.

He was talkative this time. He'd gotten married but—don't laugh, don't laugh—he was about get a divorce. Did I feature in this archeological conversation? you ask. No. But I wanted to be with him again, surrender and then vomit him up in an act of Florbellian revenge. In other words, I wanted to swim in the blue of that parallel world to which only he seemed to have the key. I grabbed his hand and brought him home. He took off in the morning, but he didn't leave me by myself. He'd deposited death in the wrong part of my body—and my psychic gifts didn't warn me, careless pragmatist that I was.

43

You couldn't forgive me for how easily I forgave. I forgave Lia for hurting you. I forgave an old, desperate friend for that fake letter he wrote to try to drive us apart. Unforgivable deeds, I know—but was it not from the unforgivable that the need for forgiveness was born? If I reminded you of this ontological evidence, you'd get mad: that's just what you needed, an atheist trying to teach you the catechism. And I'd laugh, and we'd forgive each other again.

Sometimes it seemed to me that we got into arguments just so we could enjoy the pleasure of that return to intimacy—in that sense, our anger was no different from the warriorlike doggedness of old married couples. I didn't care that you railed against my slave morality. What I couldn't take was when you accused me of getting along with people out of social convenience. Because it was completely unfair, and you didn't realize it.

When lots of people started whispering that since your entrée into politics you'd become all about strategy and special interests, I stilled their venomous tongues by singing your praises. Never, not even for a second, did your shift to expensive suits and a secretary pool to fulfill your every need make me lose sight of what you were.

I like people with an entomologist's affection, if you will. Or the mercifulness of atheists, who are better equipped to accept human fallibility. Knowing that heaven isn't protecting me helps me understand my fellows in defenselessness. I forgave one awful person the awful act of desiring the privilege of my friendship. What you may not know is that I haven't forgiven myself for having thought ill of you because of that disgraceful letter.

I should have realized immediately that you couldn't have written it, of course. Even though the handwriting was identical to yours, which it was—I know. But it's hard to hit upon the perfect amount of faith—especially when that faith is employed only as a fail-safe. Knowing that we are all capable of the very best and the very worst is useful for loving to the last drop, but it doesn't exactly help a person believe in permanent goodness. It's only now that I've discovered you were the most permanent goodness I had—and I'm endlessly grateful to you for that.

Because you died, I'm experiencing the breath of eternity for the first time—I believe now that there's a place out there where you're waiting for me. Don't smile—that's still not faith. In my mind, the place where the dead dwell is a plain of ashes. A long stretch of space suffused with the melancholy of those who refuse to let go of life, like you. A place without God—but with you.

And even if that place is just a mirage produced by my grief, life without you doesn't hurt anymore. I can drag my gouty leg—I don't need to jog by your side. I can forgo the new masterworks of cinema, dance, music, and painting—they dare to exist without you. I can renounce my parents' ragged estrangement, my mother's stabbed heart, my father's absence. Your whole family is already gone. I see our friends as ghosts of you now—people who are suddenly too young, too alive for my longing for the two of us.

44

I let myself be killed by a child who could never exist. Pascoal can't accept it—if only you could make him see that I'm the only one to blame. I avoided the hypothetical unpleasantness of his split with Augusto. I was more and more a friend of the world, less and less the friend of any one person. I strove to fix the world's problems, addicted to my planetary good conscience—to the applause, the present-day trickle and the future waves sure to come. I took refuge in Big Action; I had no desire to see anyone who could wander through the ancient arteries of my youth.

I met Pascoal the year my parents died. He'd lost his father three years earlier. We talked so much that we started swapping nightmares: he saw my parents screaming as the car rolled over the bank, and I saw his father suffocating, his body wasted from cancer.

My father saved me from death twice. Pascoal's had never saved him, and he saw that as a bad omen. For Pascoal, the rigor of science and the exactitude of presages danced in each other's arms like diligent debutantes. You thought he was "lyrical"—yes, I know you aren't homophobic, but you always considered gays to be different. Or maybe, in Pascoal's case, you were discomfited by the remarkable resemblance between the two of you—because Pascoal was an erudite conservative, like you. To sleep easy, he needed order, his music, and the conviction that history moved in a circle.

Pascoal had never swallowed two candies at once, like I did at three years old—my father shaking me hard, grabbing me by the feet and shaking me till the candies fell to the floor, shaking me and berating the women screaming beside him, my mother and grandmother—don't you see you're just upsetting the child, you selfish women? My father slowly climbing up to the roof where I'm clinging somehow; I'm five years old and I feel my fingers give, too weak to hold my body suspended over the void, his voice frighteningly calm and sweet—

"Just hang on a little bit longer, sweetie, Daddy's coming to get you."

My father's embrace, afterward, a compact wall against my mother's nervous rage—

"Shh, shh, it's over now, Mommy's not going to spank you, I won't let her."

My father slapped me over everything and nothing, until the day I decided to ignore him, to pretend that slap had never happened—

"Mom, can you pass the salt, please?"

—and yet he loved me, and I loved his love. I loved his love and my mother's, a putrefied love with the doughy consistency of immensely trivial things. They quarreled in that love as if they wanted to be rid of it, and whenever they reached the exit, they retreated. Some days they seemed to hate each other, swelling with recriminations, hurling things through the air, shouting defiantly.

They only rarely managed to love each other at the same time; it seemed that only in rage were they in sync. I used to feel pity as I watched him flapping around her like a sparrow fallen from its nest, asking her endless questions, patting her on the back, hemming her in with pinches and tickles, with the clumsy improvisation of emotional illiterates, which the vast majority of men of that generation were. Molded for war, trained in the transparent blindness of killing, with their organs for loving sliced out. And whatever mother I still had left from his disheveled love would pass me the salt.

44

If only I had the awkward consolation of a son or daughter. With
your friend Teresa, for example. You thought she got on my nerves,
didn't you? And you were right: the only reason I didn't bicker
with her more was so I didn't have to stop bickering with you. You
brought me so many women, and the only one I was interested in
was the one you'd have considered off-limits. Your alter ego. Your
sister. My sister's sister—oh, delicious incest! Yes, I like vain, stubborn Teresa, despite her green-painted fingernails and her stridently
cheap dresses. I often fantasized about the texture of her adolescent
breasts—did you know that? They were too perfect—or maybe that's
exactly it, because people get tired of human perfection too. At least
old people do.

Teresa was constantly undergoing exterior remodeling in rebel-
lion against her unguarded interior. Teresa admired you more than
you would even be capable of—were you aware of that? And, naïvely,
she urged you not to be so hard on yourself. Teresa embraced all the
Lias and other stray dogs in your life—starting with me. I always said
she lacked *wit*—the English word seemed to cover it more neatly
than Portuguese—more to convince myself of that lack than to reas-
sure you. But what Teresa actually lacked was malice, and that made
her one of the most seductive women I ever met. She was utterly
without the snarkiness that is so fashionable these days. I think of

her now as if she no longer exists. Because even Teresa died when you died on me. You were the one who sprinkled the air around her with stars. But then dead Teresa rings my doorbell. Eager for the pleasure of my surprise.

"I was afraid you'd died too. But you're smiling. You smile like her."

"I'd say I am her."

I beg you to let me love Teresa with the now-idle tenderness I once devoted to you. For no reason. Because it was for no reason that I loved you—merely to perch on the raw diamond of your soul and discover from that vantage point my life's residual glow.

I see Teresa through your dead eyes, fires in the aftermath. I hear you inside my voice. Words charred by longing for life, words that weep like ballads, words tangled in childhood music. Crashing to the ground like windowpanes, bursting in the air like balloons, like fireworks. Maimed bears growling in pain over a glass eye that was yanked out because of love, to see what that love is made of, that warm love without which we cannot fall asleep. Teresa removes her sandals with the stupidly high heels that make her teeter through daily life, and she dances.

She's singing. Don't you hear her? She's singing all through your house. You really can't hear her?

And I dance with Teresa, in my darkening living room, as if you hadn't died on me and I could still use your heart to love. If only the angel of jealousy would snatch your skinny body back to earth and bring you to this room where Teresa is dancing in my arms. If you could see Teresa tug at my masculine desire, this pleasure sullied by my longing for you. In Teresa's flying body I remember your own flights, the flights of other women I've loved. I remember the limpid choreography with which they summoned love. That radio journalist I had such a thing for and then cheated on when she was out of town for a couple of nights, with that lost university student who looked like a mannequin—remember? And remember how, months later, the two of them collaborated to make a TV program—one that happened to have been my idea? I remember how angry you got, jealous angel, when you found me talking with the girl with the mannequin body, who turned out not to be lost at all.

"Don't you see that woman was using you?"

Yes, she was using me, Tink, just like I was using her, like we all use one another. Ultimately, that's what life is: we all use one another, as best we can. Did I use you the way I should have? Why is there still so much of you left?

45

At least I didn't leave any parents or kids behind—at least I never experienced the madness of the death of a child. The only person I abandoned was you—that's it. If you were my son, you'd have known that letter insulting you couldn't have been written by me. You sent it back to me with a curt note: "Most esteemed madam, I imagine you must have sent this to the wrong address." I didn't respond—what response could I give to that kind of nastiness? I became suspicious of all our mutual friends—and that was the thing I really couldn't forgive you for. And even after you learned the truth, when the guilty party fell gravely ill and decided to come clean, you kept protecting him. You apologized, but you refused to tell me his name.

"It's not anybody you like. Not one of your friends."

And what about liking you—what should I do with that feeling, which could evaporate with the first misstep? How could you protect a guy who went through your papers and read my letters so he could write you distorted lines that debased my signature? What kind of friendship needs to destroy other friendships in order to exist? I found out about all of it really quickly—spite travels at warp speed, you know. You didn't want to tell me who the scoundrel was, but you told Fish Stick, who then told me, in a well-meaning effort to calm me down. The inadvertent bile of good intentions.

"You demand too much of people. You want your friends to be perfect, and nobody can stand up to that kind of pressure."

No, I didn't want you all to be perfect. But I wanted friendship to be an is-land of perfection in the turbulent oceans of our lives. An island that only Teresa showed me, despite her countless faults—or through them. Proud, mouthy Teresa whom you disliked, her voice strident and her head held high, a no-parking sign—here I come. Teresa who is amazed by any hint of novelty—she was always like that, even at eighteen. Teresa who spends the money she has and even some she doesn't on clothing, beauty products, and plastic surgeries, and who likes painting the nails on her fingers and toes black or lettuce green, to your horror. Teresa who was fired from her job at the library on my say-so because I was afraid the director was considering replacing me with her. Naïve Teresa—the director chided me a few times for having hired her, but she was skilled at get-ting what she wanted. And it's not like I even wanted to stay there—the quiet work was a good fit for me when I was writing my doctoral dissertation, that's all. But Teresa liked feeling that she was sacrificing herself for me. Teresa with the non-soundproofed walls who heard my most shameful secrets with a smile of infi-nite love, without moralizing or pity. Teresa who always tried to choose first and snag the best spot—at the movies, in people's homes, in life—but shrugged her shoulders, unbothered, when we teased her about it afterward. Teresa who lent me clothing and jewelry, who used to show up at my door to turn my wardrobe inside out whenever she read in the paper that I was going to be participating in a TV debate. Teresa who provided me a bed, sleep, and cigarettes after every one of the major disappointments of my life, and who never left anything unsaid.

If Teresa had received a letter insulting her in my handwriting, she never would have believed I'd written it. She lacked wit, as you said, using the English word; she was no genius. But she had laserlike accuracy even when I was racked by doubt. She knew a lot of about the unspoken things we're made of; she had X-ray vision from navigating between lighthouses through the caves of night. And I couldn't stand hearing you run her down—I knew one day you were going to make me cry, and she'd be the one to dry my tears.

Like she's drying yours now; look—she called you a million times, got worried when you failed to answer, and here she is knocking on your door. SOS. Depression—yes, the Teresa you see as mushy and useless spends eight hours a week taking calls from hopeless people she's never met, preventing suicides, bringing light to this world that you view with such scorn. Open the door to her, go on. Give her the smile I gave you. She deserves our love, the love I bequeathed to you, threadbare love, the old gold of beauty that does not fade.

"You're smiling. You smile like her."

"I am her," you say. And I start looking at Teresa through eyes you've lent me. Teresa whom you never wanted to see and who was like a piece of me. I loved all of your pieces; I even loved that jealous old man who wrote to you pretending to be me in an effort to drive you away from me. Why? For no reason. No reason. Because it was for no reason that I loved you—I discovered in you the resplendent uselessness of my soul. In you, I discovered what I was beyond everything I'd so far been. This friendship has never known the limits of perfection or retreat. It only echoes, whispers to us, endlessly delivers us to the soil of nonexistent affinities. With my eyes that are no longer eyes, you start to see Teresa's soul—the part of Teresa that doesn't have green or black fingernails or carefully highlighted curves. Teresa now has what you are lacking, and it is the best of me, what I ceased being because I was so focused on doing.

I hear you inside my voice, words rumpled by time, words that roar like a conch shell, words that contain tumbling marbles and glassblowers' rhythmic breathing, words that restore a sound that precedes meaning. Teresa removes her high-heeled sandals and dances in the silence of your vast living room.

She's singing. Don't you hear her? She's singing all through your house. You really can't hear her?

Teresa was never able to distinguish between singing and sobbing—that's why she loved me so accurately. She didn't see me, as you did, rounding the closed loop of the roller coaster of my life. She saw me as she sees the world—perpetually being born, laughter and tears bound together in the courage of understanding. And you dance with Teresa in your dim living room, treading meringue clouds, locked in a virginal embrace, the ever-important aesthetic rules you erected as defenses now lowered. You used to bristle at me when I pointed out how intolerant you were: "Have you looked in the mirror lately? You've got that word written in red ink across your forehead, sweetheart." Sure, you couldn't stand external signs of degradation—uneducated voices, eccentric clothing, houses overrun with knickknacks, painted nails. But I was intolerant of signs of inner capitulation, and that intolerance had no cure. "Your standards are so high, one of these days you're not even going to talk to me."

Turns out you were right. And you, who talks to everybody—how many people have you talked to? The bird of jealousy flaps around the room where Teresa is dancing in your arms, singing instead of me, bathing the two of you in a purple, funereal light, which happens to be my color. I wanted to be in her place, yes, to laugh in your arms again—but it's a weightless jealousy, just a hint of the memory of jealousy, almost a nostalgia for my human fallibility.

More and more I've been lingering on the good that so often flowed invisibly over our days. For example, the day when that student of the Lusitanian essence with whom you'd patriotically cheated on your absent girlfriend rescued that girlfriend, whom you'd meanwhile dumped, from despair and perhaps from unemployment. Your ex-girlfriend, who was studying law and working at a radio station, was at the end of her rope when your ex-lover, who hosted a beauty tips program on the station, found her sobbing convulsively. She was in the grip of the Blank Page Monster only an hour out from a special on a poet who'd just died. The editor, seeing her sunk in unproductive tears, had warned her that he had stacks of résumés on his desk from young journalists eager to take her job. Finding her in that state, your former student-for-a-night sat down next to her and asked, "Will you let me help you?" She took the newspaper clippings and calmly wrote the deceased poet's biography for broadcast, including notes with suggestions for music to accompany the text.

A couple of months later, the two of them hosted a TV program that I knew to be one of your old projects: Childhoods, a set of stories about the early years of a number of celebrities. Mannequin Body ran into you one night in Bairro Alto and asked you if you'd seen the program and if you'd liked it. You put on your cherry-picker smile and told her the program had worked overall, but maybe they should switch out some of the illustrious grandmas and -pas for some emerging stock—the childhoods of young actors and actresses, young artists, young scientists. Young Mannequin Body tossed you that Comme des Garçons smile of hers and declared that youth was overvalued, given that we lived in a desert of genuine talent. Then she excused herself and went off to deliver the next install-ment of her Sahara theory to the head of a rival channel who was heading toward the dance floor.

And I fluttered off, laughing, on the scruffy back of the bird of jealousy. The devil's bird, ever interposed between God and our human frailty, its exuberant plumage the color of deception. That night, for example, I could only call it dis-appointment. I was hurt by your kindness toward that woman who'd used you, but you laughed and said we all use one another; that's the beauty of life.

In fact, on an upcoming time curve, Mannequin Body will be replaced, in the shop window of the TV screen, by another Mannequin Body. A publishing big shot decides to offer the replacement Body the chance to run a new publication called Health for Success. Mannequin Body Two accepts, eager to—as she read in Health Forever magazine and now repeats to the big shot—"develop her hidden leadership energies."

But serving on the editorial board of Triunfo.com Publications is Original Mannequin Body, a woman who'd be about sixty if she weren't waging battle against every wrinkle to remain in her forties, via periodical excursions to the magical chambers of her friend Surgeon-on-Demand. Original Mannequin Body's memory has been weakened by all those anesthetics, but she never forgets her place in the world. Most of all, she remembers the day when they told her that Mannequin Body Two was going to replace her as the anchor during prime time.

So Original Mannequin Body now explains to the owner of Triunfo.com Publications, fleeting ex-lover and eternal friend, that Mannequin Body Two doesn't have the skills to edit anything—not even a magazine that's 70 percent translated from English, as would be the case here. She says Mannequin Body Two couldn't write her way out of a paper bag; all the things she's published, to a fawning audience, were actually written by a variety of good journalists in ex-change for intimate favors. She adds that Mannequin Body Two misses deadlines, talks about people behind their backs, and has rudimentary English that doesn't go much beyond "I love you."

Triunfo.com Big Shot is taken aback by this. He recalls having seen Mannequin Body Two interviewing Michael Caine in unimpeachable English, and frowns. But Original Mannequin Body says, "Of course I don't bear the girl any ill will. When she replaced me a few years ago, it was obvious that it was the station's directive—our viewers get tired of us, want to see new faces. Anyway, as you know, I remained close friends with the station head. I even attended his wedding a few months back—it was practically a private ceremony, only a hundred and fifty guests."

Triunfo.com Big Shot manages to get a word in edgewise: "Oh, he remarried, I didn't realize."

Original Mannequin Body sighs and notes that, sadly, the marriage fell apart—the bride had to be institutionalized because of some sort of mental illness, a serious one, can you imagine. Original Mannequin Body then philosophizes at length about the difficult art of marriage and her disappointment at having failed in that area— "Deep down, you know, I'm the sentimental type." Triunfo.com Big Shot realizes that hiring Mannequin Body Two is out of the question. He tells the secretary that whenever she calls, he's not in.

And so, on an upcoming time curve, Mannequin Body Two will be unemployed. She'll turn to self-help books, where she'll learn that every crisis presents a window of opportunity (which Triunfo.com Big Shot has also read in the economics magazines he consumes) and start auditioning for TV soap operas.

Four time curves later, she'll be the one to send Original Mannequin Body to an obligatory and lonely retirement, as well as Mannequin Bodies Five and Seven (Six having been impaled on another, Portuguese-style curve, bereft of both metaphysics and Álvaro de Campos's chocolate, and become paraplegic), who, two time curves later, will get their revenge on her.

45

If only you'd let me love your child. Push him out of the bowels of your death and let me keep him with me. Allow him perhaps to sample the warmth of Teresa's breasts. Her hair that smells of fresh-mown grass—the grass that now covers you. A smell that has filled me with nostalgia for childhood ever since I was a boy.

Many returned from Africa with the heavy odor of the red soil pervading their veins. Others didn't come back; they'd become addicted to that odor and sent for their families to join them. I dreamed of the scent of mown grass at my Portuguese high school. And the scent of youth, of beginning things—a scent that not even your chain-smoked cigarettes could smother in you. Hugging Teresa, I'm a miserable twerp weeping over the child who killed you. I swaddle that stern infant, show him your smiling face in the photo. I change his diapers, talk to him about women—ultimately, I'm capable of talking only about you.

I was your choice, the intermittent victory of your freedom over your body's magnetic field, otherwise known as your friend. Allow me to enter your death.

Teresa is squeezing my fingers now. An airplane is crossing the twilit heavens above the twinkling city. You were here, just now, and you left. I talk to Teresa about how much I still miss you. We tear stories of you to shreds. We don't turn on the lights, waiting for you in the dark. In the dark of the dark of the dark.

46

I'm not going to be getting revenge on anybody—the curves of my time ran out the minute I produced that misplaced child. All children are born in the wrong place, most likely. Jesus showed me that too—his adoptive father, a gentle carpenter, loved him with more clemency than his real father, who was God.

Aren't all fathers God? The tyrannical ones, the indifferent ones, the obsessive ones, pulling us along by the bonds of blood, guilt, remorse. A God we kill when we fulfill his dreams. A God we murder slowly when we carry out his nightmares.

In the fiery red of fourteen years old, the age when parents are rejected and chosen, I no longer had parents to choose—only the noisy evidence of a couple of ghosts in the penumbra of my body.

Maybe you were the father I chose, my love on the cross—Father, Son, Holy Spirit. I didn't love you any less or more for having chosen you late, my heart subdued by interrupted dreams. Every night of the life I invented with you, I prayed that an angel would kindle your soul, an angel who resembled—oh, the vanity of love—my own prime.

In that time curve where I no longer am, there's a little girl slowly devouring me. It's pure love, the books say, and sex doesn't matter. So why does it feel like a reptile is crushing my body and my will? Why does the scent of damp earth make me weep and the seed of sadness devour my bones and split my skin open? The little girl is born, and you appear with a bouquet of white roses in your hand.

"May I love your child?"

"Love isn't something where you ask permission. But what do you know about love? If you knew, you'd wipe your feet when you came in and never leave again. You're a twerp."

"Your son's a twerp too. He's got a crushed-strawberry mouth, like his father, and that's without even knowing how to kiss yet. And his eyes too, the eyes of a sheep in a slaughterhouse. He's going to be a lot of work. And he's not going to love you better than I do."

"Reproduction only makes love worse. Like with painting. It's not good colors that make a good painter. You left me. You were my family, and you left me."

"No, I wasn't your family—I don't lend you money or split inheritances with you. Plus, I came back, and we're alive. Families only gather together for good in cemeteries. I'm your choice, the intermittent victory of your freedom over your body's magnetic field. Your friend, if you even know what that word means anymore."

"So change my son's diaper—I'm still recovering from childbirth."

And my child stops crying when you pull him onto your lap and kiss his forehead. And my son kisses your forehead, eleven time curves later, as you're dying in another bed in this same hospital where I've never been. But your fingers, thanks to the alteration of the curves of time, now nestle in Teresa's, whose nails are painted blue.

Teresa is squeezing your fingers as they will be squeezed by the immediate future that still seems immensely remote from you. An airplane crosses the twilit heavens, above the twinkling city, as it will in that moment when you take your last breath, your lungs battered by a deadly car that wasn't aiming at you, cheered by that image of me smiling at you from your bedside table. I know I'll be there, darling, to act as your God, to tell you we're going to be able to start over from scratch, rewrite the smudged notebooks of our friendship.

The sight of that time curve made the bird of jealousy fly far away. That desertion of wings leaves me cold, as if, in carrying off my jealousy, it were also *carrying off a warm piece of the flesh I no longer have. You and Teresa talk a long time, both lying on the hardwood floor, the curtains fluttering, darkening with the night that's coming in through the open window. The two of you talk about how much you miss me, failing to hear the music of my tears, light, immaterial, music that is forgotten within everything that is being, like the love songs that made my life a gentler sort of thing.*

46

I sometimes used to see you sitting in the armchair at the far end of the living room—your armchair. To prolong the illusion, I stopped turning on the light when I came in. When you disappeared, I'd close my eyes and realize you'd gone to the kitchen to get some ice for your whiskey. I could hear the cubes in the glass, your hand rattling the drink. Since Teresa's started coming around more often, escorted by Pascoal, I don't see you anymore. We talk about you a lot. Maybe for that reason, I'm starting to feel like you're no longer with us.

47

You, Teresa, Pascoal—inseparable now, packing me away through your laughter. You talk about me a lot. I exist less and less outside of your deficient imaginations. You talk about me a lot, but you don't remember my voice. When you say night, it's your night that thrums in the crowded heat you've sketched around my death. You no longer have a hard time walking into your empty house and closing the door. You smile at my photo, the transfigured memory of what I ceased to be. You're able to fall asleep without remembering the grave where my body is decaying. You live once more in mortals' frivolous immortality.

I'm in your house waiting for you, but you don't see me—a mother overcome by fatigue, spying on you from an armchair. I'm dead, but I still haven't gotten used to the idea. I was so busy painting pictures of heavenly nightclubs for destitute children—yes, Mommy's up in heaven dancing with Grandma, and now they're playing cards—I got lost on the way to the epic, monotonous paradise depicted in stained-glass windows.

I ask God to prolong this earthly stage, to appoint me as your personal angel until you come up to this cloud-filled limbo and show me the way to the final casino. Or maybe he can negotiate with the Hindu gods and get me placed back on earth as your dog. Or cat. Or at least your canary. Gratitude is a way of life in which I'd be spared the howls of pain of those who die. I imagine God must be swamped with emergencies. I burrow into your walls. I say: clarity; and you repeat, dreaming: clarity. I say: blood of my breath; and you repeat: blood of my breath. I say: I'm here; and you reply with: absence.

47

I list the laws of the thermodynamics of your absence. Number one: acceleration. I can drive as fast as I want now, without your furious panic getting in my way. Few pleasures surpass this one, driving recklessly along the seashore on a summer night, with the windows down and the music turned all the way up (you did like that part, but it's impossible to listen to loud music without stepping on the gas pedal).

Number two: energy moves from warmer zones to colder ones. Your David Bowie shouts at the heavens looking for life on Mars—I picture your good Lord with his hair standing on end, and then I see you, smiling at me, with hot-pink robes and two ribbons instead of wings, above a drunken convertible that's zigzagging toward me. But you snatch up the car and hurl it over a wall; I hear it smash onto the rocks as you disappear in the moonlight. I dial emergency services, and I forgive you again.

48

I'm with you in the place of death, tracing the impetuous curves of the coast road. We're being passed by flying motorcycles, David Bowie is on the car stereo asking whether there's life on Mars, and you roll down the window and breathe in the smell of the sea air, the light spilling intermittently onto the waves. You turn up the volume on the stereo; the girl with the mousy hair looks for her invisible friend, and above a furious piano there's a lawman beating up the wrong guy, Mars's impossible life expanding and accelerating a bit more. Watch out—there's a convertible careening across the road toward us, a drunk driver about to take you out as part of his suicide.

Please, God, don't mix up the curves of time again. There's a teenage girl up ahead who needs my friend's life. The drunk sails over the wall and smashes onto the rocks alone; this God you don't believe in sped up his crash to keep you on this side of life a little longer.

48

Incompetent murderer, where did you carry my dead friend off to? That drunk dickhead had a family, and I feel guilty for having escaped his fate. If he'd crashed into me, maybe he would have lived. I was almost free of you. And here I am, newly condemned to the dense weight of waiting. Lady Death is amusing herself by turning me into a mail carrier or, best-case scenario, a high-end spectator. Growing old consists of this miserable art of dodging: tallying one's dead, sucking in one's belly, and taking a deep breath.

49

I used to imagine you so much, once I stopped seeing you. I never wrote a bill without thinking about your ethical reservations. And about commas—your obsession with proper comma usage: "They sprinkle them around willy-nilly nowadays, like pearls. Pearls for swine, obviously. These turkeys don't even go by ear. Totally ignorant. Whatever. I'm the ignorant one. People these days are proud of their ignorance." You used to grumble a lot. You always stopped short at the door of the mythical "in my time" because I refused to let you enter the unwary claustrophobia of that hall of distorted mirrors. "Your time is now, dickhead," I'd tell you, turning your vocabulary back on you. Your time is still now, dickhead—stop dwelling on the harsh things you said to me in the past. What I now see with absolute clarity isn't words—I see that ageless day when we will once more start to live a story in which happiness isn't a pretext for martyrdom.

History isn't circular, my friend, as that ancient sect claims. If the curves of time didn't take unpredictable paths, you would have ended up moving in with Teresa and later, encouraged and assisted by her, publishing an essay titled "The Premonition of Europe." And you'd have dedicated to me what would have been the first of many books that we would no longer write together, and which would have made you a more useful and prominent figure than me.

I don't need to tell stories anymore. I've dropped all the shiny effects and reached the very heart of love, that thick ink that flows across time's surface and *transforms everything it touches. It might be a crumpled word, a wilting flower, a conch shell in which the sea where I no longer dwell still glitters. It might be your face yesterday, or what's left of it today. What matters isn't the plot, the form, not even the color. What matters is the unified circulation of a body and a soul around the bare sediment of their truth.*

49

Teresa came across an article of mine in a drawer. She suggests I write more about that "incandescent dream of Europe" I discussed with you so often. The dream of the ultimate center, which loves other centers insofar as they are suburbs of itself. "At least in Portugal," you used to say, with that glorious laugh of yours, "we don't have that problem: we're used to seeing ourselves as the suburb of all of Europe. Which means we see ourselves as Ali Baba's secret cave." And then I'd hold forth on how those tendencies fostered arrogance or timidity, unease or fatalism.

And after you left, I'd write a long screed about the human epidemic, Portuguese in origin, of folding the world smaller and smaller until it matches our diminutive dreams. Or of expanding our nightmares to the epic scale of a pocket-size memory. I held forth on the humility with which nationalistic movements irrigated themselves until they eventually burst forth like oceans of pride. But I don't have the heart to write anymore. I've been asked for an article on the history of Portuguese ceramics, and I lack that eager interest in minor arts that glinted in your black tile eyes. I lack, in general, your excitable, anti-geometric perspective, which distorted shapes like the 3-D glasses created for the horror films of my youth.

Maybe I could write a whole book on Teresa's skin, like Voltaire, who used his lover's back as a desk. Maybe, like you, I could camouflage the contours of the solitude you've left me in.

50

Quick. The girl has dropped her books in the street, and the car won't have time to brake. Quick—hurl yourself at her. You can save someone this time. You're not going to redeem your platoon-mate's death; death doesn't ask for redemption. Death doesn't ask for anything, my dear—don't worry. Life alone points its finger at you, the life of human beings as imperfect as you, heroic and bumbling, camouflaging their original blindness with overweening certainty. Come on, don't be scared, leap at that girl who's smiling at you like me, and save her. I'm waiting for you in a place where words no longer hurt, no longer wound, are neither in excess nor lacking. That place does exist.

50

And suddenly you've come back. Your running looks like flying, with that furious weightlessness unique to adolescence. The red ribbon dances atop your tousled hair. You're carrying a wobbly stack of books in your arms, and your white sandals barely touch the ground. There's a fog of dense heat pressing down on everything, but your smile penetrates that fog, shatters it, drags the blue of the sky through the city streets. Your books spill out in the middle of the road, and you kneel down to pick them up, still smiling. You forget to curse. Yes, it's you. Your smile advancing steadily across my face. It's you before I met you. That's why you're not upset, why you're unfazed by everything. Kneeling on the asphalt, you calmly gather each book. Some pages come loose and soar off. You chase after them without losing that smile.

"Watch out, Tink. Run!"

But I'm the one suddenly running in a dream of flight. I shove you into the past, your lithe body leaps toward life at the last moment, I still hear the squeal of the car's desperate braking. You enter into my flesh, pound against doors and windows, smash me into the glass. And I see you there below, now racing through the garden, the red ribbon in your hair lighting up the green lawn. There will be a whiff of lost youth in that lawn, a scent that comes out only when the grass is wet. But I no longer remember what it was like—it's far off in the distance, moving farther and farther away.

About the Author

Photo © Alfredo Cunha

Born in 1962, Inês Pedrosa earned a degree in communication sciences from the Universidade NOVA de Lisboa before earning several journalism awards through her work in the press, on the radio, and on television. Her weekly column in the Portuguese national newspaper *Expresso* was awarded the 2007 Prize for Parity for Citizenship and Gender Equality. She currently contributes to two culture-focused radio shows and a public television show and also works as a literary translator (notably of the work of Milan Kundera). In 2017, she founded her own publishing house, Sibila. She is the author of *In Your Hands* (Pedrosa's English-language debut and winner of the 1997 Prémio Máxima de Literatura in Portugal); *A eternidade e o desejo* (*Eternity and Desire*, finalist for the 2009 Portugal Telecom Award and the 2010 Prémio Correntes d'Escritas); and *Os íntimos* (*The Intimates*, winner of the 2012 Prémio Máxima de Literatura). For more information about the author, visit www.inespedrosa.com.

About the Translator

Photo © Karla Rosenberg

Andrea Rosenberg translates texts from both Spanish and Portuguese. Her full-length translations include Inês Pedrosa's *In Your Hands*, Tomás González's *The Storm*, Aura Xilonen's *The Gringo Champion*, Juan Gómez Bárcena's *The Sky over Lima*, and David Jiménez's *Children of the Monsoon*. She holds an MFA in literary translation and an MA in Spanish from the University of Iowa, and she has been the recipient of awards and grants from the Fulbright Program, the American Literary Translators Association, and the Banff International Literary Translation Centre.